LEFT

TO

ENVY

(An Adele Sharp Mystery—Book Six)

BLAKE PIERCE

Blake Pierce

Blake Pierce is the USA Today bestselling author of the RILEY PAGE mystery series, which includes seventeen books. Blake Pierce is also the author of the MACKENZIE WHITE mystery series, comprising fourteen books; of the AVERY BLACK mystery series, comprising six books; of the KERI LOCKE mystery series, comprising five books; of the MAKING OF RILEY PAIGE mystery series, comprising six books; of the KATE WISE mystery series, comprising seven books; of the CHLOE FINE psychological suspense mystery, comprising six books; of the JESSE HUNT psychological suspense thriller series, comprising fifteen books (and counting); of the AU PAIR psychological suspense thriller series, comprising three books; of the ZOE PRIME mystery series, comprising six books; of the ADELE SHARP mystery series, comprising ten books (and counting); of the EUROPEAN VOYAGE cozy mystery series, comprising six books (and counting); of the new LAURA FROST FBI suspense thriller, comprising three books (and counting); of the new ELLA DARK FBI suspense thriller, comprising three books (and counting); and of the new A YEAR IN EUROPE cozy mystery series, comprising three books (and counting).

An avid reader and lifelong fan of the mystery and thriller genres, Blake loves to hear from you, so please feel free to visit www.blakepierceauthor.com to learn more and stay in touch.

BOOKS BY BLAKE PIERCE

A YEAR IN EUROPE
A MURDER IN PARIS (Book #1)
DEATH IN FLORENCE (Book #2)
VENGEANCE IN VIENNA (Book #3)

ELLA DARK FBI SUSPENSE THRILLER
GIRL, GONE (Book #1)
GIRL, TAKEN (Book #2)
GIRL, HUNTED (Book #3)

LAURA FROST FBI SUSPENSE THRILLER
ALREADY GONE (Book #1)
ALREADY SEEN (Book #2)
ALREADY TRAPPED (Book #3)

EUROPEAN VOYAGE COZY MYSTERY SERIES
MURDER (AND BAKLAVA) (Book #1)
DEATH (AND APPLE STRUDEL) (Book #2)
CRIME (AND LAGER) (Book #3)
MISFORTUNE (AND GOUDA) (Book #4)
CALAMITY (AND A DANISH) (Book #5)
MAYHEM (AND HERRING) (Book #6)

ADELE SHARP MYSTERY SERIES
LEFT TO DIE (Book #1)
LEFT TO RUN (Book #2)
LEFT TO HIDE (Book #3)
LEFT TO KILL (Book #4)
LEFT TO MURDER (Book #5)
LEFT TO ENVY (Book #6)
LEFT TO LAPSE (Book #7)
LEFT TO VANISH (Book #8)
LEFT TO HUNT (Book #9)
LEFT TO FEAR (Book #10)

CHAPTER ONE

Dawn introduced itself with interloping rays of gold through the multicolored glass, hiding *things* in the shadows of the archways. The sunlight scattered the colors from the stained glass windows across the long, swirling, circular mosaic floors. Docent Vicente stood behind the cordoned velvet ropes, one hand resting against the wooden privacy partition and his other resting delicately on the cool, silver knob of a queue divider. He smiled from where he stood in the threshold of the structure. For ten years, he'd been providing tours through the heart of culture itself, and yet every day he felt the same sensation of wonder as the first time he'd set foot in the Sistine Chapel.

More than half a millennium in age, heralding stories of a time past but also suggesting of others to come. Not just the masterwork paintings, or the mosaic craftsmanship, but also a sense of holiness, of awe.

He stood in the doorway, peering along the ground, breathing softly to himself and murmuring a quiet Latin prayer—a morning ritual before every tour. A small consecration, an offering to join the many voices lifted up over the centuries.

Vicente heard movement and he turned, smoothing the front of his uniform and glancing along the hall, in the opposite direction of the main room.

A custodian was pushing a small red bucket on wheels, a mop angled and brushing the man's shoulder. Vicente smiled and gave a little wave, still murmuring the prayer beneath his breath.

"*Saluto.* Ready for the day?" the custodian asked.

Vicente racked his brain. Timothe, he recalled. This was the man's name, yes? Yes.

He paused the cadence of his prayer for a moment and adjusted his sleeves. "*Buongiorno,* Timothe," he said, pausing, looking for a reaction. Nothing apparent, suggesting he'd correctly remembered the name. "Ready for our visitors?"

The custodian grunted, silver keys jingling where he pulled them and began finagling with a small supply closet tucked behind the

1

entrance foyer. Not all history could be perfectly maintained—some additions, perhaps. But not to the heart of it all.

"Tourists arriving soon," said Timothe. "My work is done."

"And good work, too," said Docent Vicente. "Today will be a special day. I can feel it."

"Special—I hope. Perhaps this means no one will stick gum on the walls this time. Nor spill orange juice in the chapel."

Vicente bit his lip at the mere thought. He huffed a breath, shaking his head. "I certainly hope not. Good day!"

The custodian waved vaguely, stowing his supplies and then moving off, away from the doors leading into the heart of the chapel.

For his part, Vicente turned. He felt a niggling sensation of unease at the thought of gum or orange juice anywhere in the chapel. They had strict rules about food.

The sensation of worry turned into an itch, somewhere just near the base of his neck, prickling along his spine. Muttering darkly to himself, Vicente turned and strode through the wooden divider for the first time, beneath the refracted, multicolored light. He strode beneath the site of the rectangular paintings, swirling about the room and to the *Drunkenness of Noah*. His gaze swept the cordoned areas. No sign of juice or gum, at least. The custodians, perhaps, had done their job the night before.

He made a mental note to remind the tourists this morning of the food policy. The way some people treated history itself...

He shook his head, turning away now.

And then stopped.

A small pool of juice dappled the mosaic floor, just beneath the painting in the ceiling of David and Goliath.

He stared, blinked. A droplet fell, crimson, stippling the smooth ground and speckling the lip of the wall. He frowned, leaning in closer. He murmured the quiet Latin prayer, shaking his head as he did.

Cherry juice?

No. Too thick.

He blinked as another droplet fell as if from the sky itself, tapping against the already formed pool of red. Vicente turned slowly, with much care. He twisted and looked up.

There, hidden in the shadows of an arch, against *Judith and Holofernes* which hadn't been visible from the wooden divider, he spotted a dark form.

2

A sudden chill erupted down his spine. His arms prickled and his mouth went dry.

"H-hello?" he called. A demon was on the ceiling!

But no. A second later, he realized. Not a demon. A person. A person suspended by wires and hooks.

A corpse stuck to the ceiling of the Sistine Chapel.

Vicente stared, peering up as lifeless eyes glared back, hooks through flesh sent more droplets of red splattering to the ground, and taut metal wires gouged into the ceiling itself.

Only then, as he stared at the horrific image, did Vicente stumble back, nearly slipping on the blood, shouting as loud as any brimstone priest, "Timothe! Timothe! Call the police!"

CHAPTER TWO

Seven days earlier...

Adele moved with quick, sure-footed steps along the garden path of the Parc Monceau back in Paris. Her breathing came slow, regimented, careful. She found some of the air a strained gasp...

This should have been her first warning.

Adele moved closer to the new crime scene. The new piece of brutal art added to the portfolio of her mother's killer. As she drew closer, crossing the caution-tape boundary, her heart hammered some more. She found it difficult to breathe.

This should have been her second warning.

She came to a halt, staring at the corpse.

Fingers missing. A lacework of cuts and curling wounds, like some horrendous painting slashed into the flesh of the young woman. Marion Elise Ramon. A coincidence her middle name matched Adele's mother's? Unlikely. Even the wounds, the missing fingers, the brutal torture matched Elise Romei's own crime scene. Also found on the side of a running trail in a quiet park, left to be discovered.

Adele started hyperventilating. For a moment, she felt like she couldn't draw breath. She stared, her body starting to tremble, to shake, from her thighs, to her stomach, up her chest and arms. Her whole form shook in the park, though the weather was mild and she'd only been strolling.

The shaking grew so bad, her gasping worsened so she couldn't look. She tore her gaze away.

"Agent Sharp?" a voice called from near the crime scene. "Agent Sharp, are you—"

She ignored it, turning, still shaking. For a moment, it felt like her knees would collapse. She'd never had a panic attack before. At least, not one this powerful. She found tears slipping down her cheeks for no reason at all. She took a stumbling step away from the crime scene, then another. Images of her own mother suddenly appeared in her mind, flashing across her eyes.

4

"Agent Sharp?" the voice called.

She ignored it, stumbling away, fleeing, faster, faster. As she moved away from the crime scene, the shaking grew easier. The pain in her chest lessened. She found she could begin to breathe again by the time she reached the car.

Gasping, trembling now, she threw herself into the vehicle and pulled away... refusing to look back...

Seven days had passed since that walk in the park in Paris.

Her breathing had improved, the shakings were gone—mostly. But the images remained.

Adele sat with her head against the white-painted wall of her bedroom back in Germany. She shivered as the images continued to whir across her eyes, though she'd closed them. She clenched, squeezing her eyes shut, trying to blockade the cavalcade of horrendous imaginings. A week since she'd visited that crime scene. A week since the memories had bobbed to the surface.

Now, she was in Germany. She'd fled France and the pressure that came with her job.

She opened her eyes, leaning back on her old bed. The last time she'd slept in this room had been nearly two decades ago. Her father's house creaked like she remembered; sometimes, the floorboards protesting movement as her father made his way around the kitchen and living room downstairs. Other times, the roof and the walls, seemingly of their own accord, groaned with old age.

Adele sighed where she lay, her eyes fixated on the low ceiling of her childhood room. The bed was firmer than she remembered. But even some of her old, less-loved stuffed animals remained, sitting on a small chest against the opposite wall. The same desk, the same paint color, the same bed—everything the same. The only difference was the new metal lock on the inside of her door. All the bedrooms had them now after the home invasion where her father had nearly died.

Then, the killer had also seemed connected to her mother's death. Again, back in this house, history seemed to be repeating itself.

There was little doubt in Adele's mind the killer of Marion Elise Ramon was a copycat. The details were too specific. Even the torturous wounds matched the same carnage wrought on Elise all those years ago. Plus the name—the middle name. The killer was taunting her. She'd kicked a hornet's nest, visiting a chocolate bar factory a few

5

weeks ago. Asking questions.

And now, she had the killer's response. Another woman butchered in an empty park.

Though her eyes were now open, the same images flashed across her mind. *Bleeding... bleeding... always bleeding.*

She saw her own mother, pictures from that crime scene playing like a slideshow through her subconscious. She shivered and rolled in the bed, facing the blue wall as if to block out the procession of horror.

The thoughts had chased her from France to Germany.

Medical leave. Mental health.

Adele actually winced at the memory of speaking to Foucault, requesting time off. He'd been more than understanding, but her own pride had taken a hit. What did the others think of her? Agent Paige? John? Robert?

She should have dived headfirst into the case—gone after the killer. But... but she simply hadn't been able to. For a week now, she felt weakened, beleaguered. An exhaustion and fatigue she'd rarely felt before. Once, perhaps. Depression, they'd said. After her mother's death.

Now, she was squarely back in the horrible, dark, lonely room of her own mind.

Back in her father's house. The two of them hadn't really even reconciled yet, not after he'd concealed information on her mother's case. The same case now haunting her. But she'd had nowhere else to go, and, to his credit, he hadn't turned her away. They'd even managed a couple of cordial conversations over bowls of soup—about anything besides work.

As if summoning him with thought alone, Adele heard the creak of the stairs outside her room. She jarred, blinking, looking over at her closed door.

Knuckles knocked quietly.

She shivered.

"Adele?" her father said. She'd flat out refused to be called by her last name any longer, and, though it had taken some getting used to, her father had finally relented.

"Busy," she called to the door.

"Just—just checking. Are you all right?"

Adele drew her blanket up around her shoulders, her eyes sealed shut for a moment, staving off a sudden headache.

"Fine… I'm fine," she said.

"Look, Adele, I—I…" Her father stumbled over the words. "It's been a week. You've barely left your room. I just wanted to—"

"We had dinner together last night," she retorted, frowning now.

"That was two nights ago, Adele. I'm beginning to worry about you."

Adele breathed slowly, feeling a flutter of unease in her chest. Even the thought of fear seemed to bring it raging back for no reason at all. She quelled the sense and exhaled through her nose, breathing slowly. "I'm fine, Dad. It's fine."

Another long, awkward pause. For a moment, she thought perhaps he'd left, though she hadn't heard his footsteps on the stairs.

Then he spoke rapidly, as if worried he might not get the words out. "Look, Adele, if this is about your mother's case…"

She rolled her eyes up and puffed a geyser of exasperated breath at the ceiling. "Damn it, Dad—not now. I said I'm busy." She felt a flash of regret at the words. Was she being harsh? It was hard to tell. Confusion was part of the panic, she'd been told. Still, just in case, she added, "Sorry. Look, I'd love to chat in an hour. Would that be okay? We can watch TV or something."

Her father seemed relieved at this olive branch and cleared his throat—a muffled, gurgling sound through the wooden door. "Great, sounds great, Sharp—er, Adele. Yes. I'll make some chowder soup."

Then, mercifully, at last, she heard his retreating footsteps moving back down the stairs and leaving her to her solace.

Adele breathed again, in for five seconds, out for seven, slow, calm…

Her father was the only other person who understood the pain, the horror of it all. He processed it in other ways, but there was something about grief that required company.

Adele sighed, sitting up now and massaging her head. She felt a shuddering headache where she sat, and blinked. For six days now, languishing around the house, she didn't feel better for it. She felt stuck, like a car in mud, spinning its wheels.

John Renee had offered some words earlier in the week, speaking from his own past of loss and pain. But she didn't need a shrink. Every *other* area with John seemed to be stuck also. Maybe even in the same mud pit. Except in that circumstance, instead of a car, she felt like a stick. Completely helpless.

7

"Christ," she muttered, remembering their last conversation.

"...Are you sure?" he'd said, his voice over the phone. *"If there's anything I can do..."*

"No, John," she'd said, in the same bed she now found herself in, watching videos on her phone. *"Maybe... maybe I need some space. It's all so heavy."*

"Right," he said. *"Space."*

"I think"—she had coughed—*"I think maybe we need to back off, you know? What do you think?"*

"Sounds appropriate. All right, Adele. If there's anything you need."

That had been the last she'd spoken with her partner. She'd worried that by asking for space, he'd want to do the opposite. John Renee was notorious for defying expectations. But he'd actually respected her words. She appreciated this at the least. Some battles were best fought alone. John wouldn't understand—he couldn't.

Adele sighed again in frustration, lying in bed. She wasn't sure what else to do—it felt like she'd curled up, allowing her emotions to pummel her, ganging up with her thoughts.

Just then, a quiet buzzing sound emanated from the chest across from her bed.

She blinked and looked over, spotting a glowing blue light, then groaned.

For a moment, she considered ignoring the phone. But then, deciding whoever was on the other end couldn't be worse than her own subconscious, she got up, still groaning, and, with what felt like lead in her feet, she stumbled over to the chest and snagged the phone.

"What?" she said.

"Hello, Adele," said a familiar voice.

She sighed softly now. "Hey, Robert."

Her old mentor and friend was just another one of the dishes waiting to be served from the back burner of calamity. Terminally ill. Yet he'd gone back to work during treatments. A few months left, perhaps a year? Maybe more.

She sighed as another jolt of sheer despair rattled her dwindling form.

"My dear, how are you?"

"I'm fine—how are you?"

"Marvelous. I have a job for you."

Adele blinked. Frowned. Then cursed, loud. "Damn it, Robert. Did Foucault put you up to this?"

Her mentor cleared his throat delicately on the other side. "No, dear. No, of course not. It was a... *mutual* consideration." Then, in a gentler, more personable tone, he said, "You can't tell me you don't want to get out of the house, dear. It's been a week. Your father called Agent Renee yesterday. Said he was worried. Said you've been cooped up—"

"He did what?" she said, finding some of the anxiety in her chest replaced by a surge of fury. "Damn it. How does he even have John's number?"

"I don't know, dear," Robert said in a tone suggesting he would have patted her cheek if they'd been in the same room.

"Damn it. Foucault knows I'm on leave."

Robert swallowed delicately. "He seemed to believe that if I called, you might be more willing to listen."

"A job? It's not—"

"No! Not that one, of course not. Foucault is industrious, not cruel. No. A different job."

"Robert, no. No—I'm sorry, I can't."

"Adele, they're asking for you specifically."

"And I'm refusing, specifically."

Robert huffed in frustration on the other end. For the normally even-tempered Frenchman this was as good as a scream. "This is a career-maker, Adele. They're asking for you specifically. Understand? The others involved are in over their heads."

"A career-maker? Sounds like more stress, Robert. I don't think—"

"Adele, you're a hunter. Hunters need to hunt. Not hunting isn't going to stress you out less—it'll make things *worse*. Do what you were made to do! Not in France," he added quickly. "I understand. But... But they're asking for you, Adele. Do you know how rare that is?"

She sighed, gnawing on her lip. All sorts of thoughts flashed through her mind. Robert was ill. Did she really want to disappoint him? Besides, her career mattered to her. It mattered to her family's legacy. It mattered for more reasons than she even could properly articulate.

In a numb, quiet voice, she murmured, "Where is it?"

"You're interested."

9

"Tell me where first."

"The Sistine Chapel."

Adele hesitated, her eyebrows inching closer for a moment. Now, a niggling in her mind arose over the other emotions. A feeling recently foreign but which she recognized now as burgeoning curiosity. Even a bloodhound with a cold still yearned for a scent to chase. This wasn't the same as the case in France, was it? This case would be in the Vatican, far away from the prying eyes of DGSI employees. Far away from it all. Practically a vacation. She winced. What could it hurt to hear Robert out? Just to listen, that was all. She didn't have to take the case.

Adele breathed softly, and then, with a roll of her eyes, she said, "I'm not agreeing. No, don't smile. I can *hear* you smiling. Just tell me about the case."

CHAPTER THREE

Adele felt the cool glass of the phone against her cheek and closed her eyes in her dark, dingy upstairs room. She exhaled slowly. "I read about this one," she said. "Details were scant. But was the victim on hooks? Dangling from the ceiling."

"Just so. Hooks in flesh, but a noose around the neck," said Robert on the other line. He spoke softly, but she detected a hint of zeal in his tone. Much like a fisherman, he seemed to realize she'd taken the bait. Her old mentor knew her well enough that if one thing could override despair, at least temporarily, it would be her own natural curiosity and desire for justice.

"I read about another one a few days ago—that one at Notre Dame. Connected?"

"We believe so. Same sort of thing. Body suspended from the ceiling by hooks. Also hung. There was a riddle."

"Hang on, a riddle?"

"The killer left a clue in Notre Dame where he would strike next. Did the same in the Sistine Chapel."

"And the clue is a riddle?"

"I'll send them to you with the case files."

Adele sighed. "He's playing a game, then? Notre Dame, and then the Sistine Chapel? How's he getting in?"

"Not sure yet. They're calling him the Tourist, some of them are calling him the Monument Killer. No name has quite stuck yet."

"Yuck."

"Precisely."

"Well... haven't been to Italy in a while."

Robert chuckled on the other end, but then burst into a round of coughing. Adele felt a flash of pain in her heart at the mere sound.

"Are you okay?" she said, reflexively.

He quickly covered, though, by muting his microphone and then, a few moments later, his voice weaker, he said, "Fine, fine. Look, Adele, I'm glad you're on board." He paused. "You *are* on board, aren't you?"

She murmured a quiet oath, but then nodded in her empty room. "I guess. This once."

"*Excellente!* I'll send the case files over immediately."

"Tickets already booked?"

"You know they are."

Adele rolled her eyes. "Thanks, Robert. Talk to you later."

He bid farewell and then they hung up. For a moment, Adele stood next to the chest at the foot of her bed, listening to the creaking house. She could hear her father from below, humming softly through the floorboards—likely near the kitchen by the sound of things. She glanced at the light switch on her wall. Her father had insisted she turn off the lights to conserve electricity. But even the Sergeant had eased up a little. At least this time he didn't ask her to squeegee the shower door after use.

Still, it would be nice to leave Germany. Leave a house full of memories. Then again, most of her memories would come with her, carry-on. This new case, though, hopefully it would distract.

She waited for her phone to buzz, glanced at the flight itinerary, and then began moving around the room, packing the few items she'd brought with her.

***

Adele had the whole row to herself as she leaned back in the economy seat, and her eyes scanned her laptop. Normally, her partner-in-crime, John Renee, would be seated next to her, likely scarfing peanuts or snoring so loudly she couldn't focus. Now, though, the seats next to her felt conspicuously… *empty.*

The crime scene photos were horrific enough. As Robert had described, the victims had been hung by a noose—wrapped around a column in one instance and through an ornamental slot in an arch in another. Hooks also stretched from the rope, looped through the victims' flesh. The hooks seemed used to put the victims' bodies in strange poses. Like the figure of Christ, the Sistine Chapel victim had his arms stretched out, the hooks gouged through his palms, holding his hands aloft. But the first victim, at Notre Dame—the hooks had been used to clasp the man's hands together beneath his chin, as if in the prayers of a silent corpse.

Adele flicked through the digital images with a rising sense of unease and disgust. She shivered as she stared and felt the plane around her rattle and shudder a bit from turbulence. The killer had already made it clear he would strike again. In the first crime scene, at Notre Dame, he'd left a riddle, mentioning things like *glass stained* and *all roads bled...* Looking at it now, it hinted at the Sistine Chapel.

Papal regret sings in glass
Stained in martyrs and saints
The noble souls feast or fast
All roads bled in paints

It wasn't clear and, in Adele's—admittedly biased—perspective, the killer was a bit wordy and full of himself. Still, the first riddle was no longer of much use, except in interpreting the second one.

This new riddle, this new clue, held Adele's attention even more.

The newest one, found at the last crime scene.

She moved away from the crime scene photos of death suspended in architectural beauty, and now read the second riddle in the file Robert had sent. A small, handwritten thing in crimson letters, transposed.

The high place of the Great
never the Virgin's fault
met an empire's fate
pillars of nations fall

Adele reread the riddle, frowning as she did. Without knowing the next crime scene, it was far more difficult to place the location. But the killer was playing games—this was clear. Games that Adele didn't wish to participate in. Robert had taught her never to engage on *their* level. But sometimes, one didn't have a choice.

Still, riddles were fine, but she'd caught killers before without the help. For all she knew, it was a distraction, an intentional, contrived attempt to dissuade the investigation.

Curious, though—certainly curious. Foucault had known what he was doing when he'd used Robert to reach out to her. The case was too interesting, too strange. He'd known she would take it—come out of hiding.

Adele sighed and flipped to the next document, wiggling a bit and rubbing her shoulders against the rough cloth covering of her economy backrest. She winced, trying to find a more comfortable position. Then, as she settled, she scanned the next item in the document.

The victims' descriptions. In Notre Dame, a German tourist—with little else of note. The Sistine Chapel victim, though, was an American cardinal visiting from New York. No connection between them as far as Adele could tell.

Both crime scenes, though, high-profile cathedrals now turned to museums. Tourist spots, but also historical spots. The press was calling this new killer the Monument Killer. But Adele felt this was a hasty assumption that the killer was choosing the locations because of some itinerant desire for spectacle. The places had other things in common: deeply religious, historically rich.

So what was the motive in it all?

She clicked back to the riddle and read it again. *"The high place of the Great..."* she murmured softly to herself, blinking as she thought.

It wasn't clear to her. But she had a sinking suspicion that if she didn't hurry, the killer would make it clear enough. This case was a career-maker, according to Robert. A vindication of all she'd been through. A vindication not only for herself, but her family. More than that, they'd asked for her specifically.

Adele felt a sudden chill at the thought. She gritted her teeth. Some cases were reputation-makers. Others were reputation-killers. Was this really the smartest move? Taking a career-maker while in the midst of a panic attack? What if she had another meltdown? What if the killer was too clever for her this time? He was wordy, obnoxious, evil—yes. But clearly also clever and shrewd. Perhaps even cleverer than any killer she'd yet faced.

Then again, it was too late to back out now. She'd already placed her career on the altar, and a knife hovered high above it, ready to plunge deep.

CHAPTER FOUR

Adele reached the front of the Leonardo Da Vinci International Airport in Rome and peered through the glass partition, waiting. She could just vaguely glimpse, past the open runways, the reflection of blue from the Tyrrhenian Sea in the coastal distance. Then she watched a slim black vehicle pull up to the curb and a few moments later, her phone buzzed, displaying an unknown number with a single word: *"Outside."*

She glanced again at the text on her phone, and then moved through the sliding doors to the pickup lane of the terminal. As she did, she frowned slightly. Robert had told her that her partner for the case would pick her up. She'd simply assumed it would be John. But the number was unknown.

A new partner?

The window to the black vehicle rolled down and a hand lifted slowly in a gesture of greeting. As the hand lowered, though, Adele nearly fell over.

She instantly felt quite self-conscious about her frazzled hair from the flight. She adjusted her sleeves and smoothed the front of her shirt subconsciously.

The man inside the car was the single most handsome person she'd ever met. She stared through the open window, and the man smiled politely.

"Ciao. Agent Sharp?" he asked in an Italian accent.

The man had a sharp, masculine jaw, completely clean shaven. His hair was parted to the side and trimmed short on the edges, also neat, tidy. His eyes were a rare blue—like moonlight trapped in winter frost. His nose was straight and firm, his lips…

Adele didn't linger long on his lips. He looked like a Calvin Klein model. Suddenly, disappointment at John not being there didn't seem so important after all.

"And you are?" she asked, leaning in just a bit to hear him better, and also to get a closer look. She'd known Italy had marble statues, she just hadn't expected one to pick her up from the airport.

"Christopher Leoni. *Agenzia Informazioni e Sicurezza Esterna.*"

Adele blinked. "AISE? Not Interpol?"

He shook his head. "We have a working relationship, I'm told. I'm here to take you to the crime scene." He spoke English nearly perfectly, with just the right amount of an accent that Adele resisted the urge to pinch herself. She was suddenly very glad she hadn't refused this case.

"Er, yeah," she said, clearing her throat and brushing her blonde hair behind an ear. "Sounds good. Just let me put my things in the trunk."

Once she had, she moved around the car and sidled into the front passenger seat. As she did, she detected the faint odor of cologne and soap. Not overpowering, especially since the window was open, but a pleasant, soft odor. Even up close, Agent Leoni looked like a man who valued tidiness. Even the inside of his car was immaculate. The dashboard shone as if polished, the floor mats were freshly vacuumed, or so it seemed. The glass displays had no hint of dust.

"How was your trip, Agent Sharp?" asked the handsome Italian.

Adele glanced over, but didn't look long, lest he suspect her of staring. The Italian agent pulled the vehicle away from the curb and moved smoothly through traffic.

"Fine. No complaints. I appreciate you taking the time to pick me up," Adele said, mostly because she couldn't think of anything else to mention.

Agent Leoni nodded once, a polite, understated gesture. "The Vatican has its own authorities," he said. "They must really need the help to ask for you specifically."

Adele paused for a moment. She'd been considering this ever since Robert had told her—why ask for her by name? Then again, over the past year or so, she had been making a bit of a name for herself in the agencies based on her closure record. For some reason, this didn't give her the small surge of pride she would've expected. Rather, she felt a bout of nerves twisting in her belly.

"Interpol has been trying something new," she said. "I'm just happy to be a part of it."

"You flew in from Germany? Another case?"

Adele hesitated. "Not a case, no. I have family there."

He continued driving through traffic, and then, in perfect German, he said, "Do you speak German too?"

She smiled at this and replied in the same language. "Yes, actually, I do. I'm surprised you do though."

The corner of his lip turned up into a coy smile. Instead of addressing her assertion, he continued in German, "Perhaps the Vatican was right to call you in. We have already cleared out the tourists, and the docent who found the body is there, along with the custodian." He transitioned back into English. "We're headed there now."

Adele was struck by how flawless his accent was. For a moment, she wondered if perhaps Agent Leoni had lived in other countries as well. For another moment, she thought of John, and his fumbling, stumbling way with any language other than French. There was nothing strained about the way Leoni spoke.

She shook her head and glanced out the window, watching the passing cars on the gray roads.

After they moved off the highway, away from the coast and through the flat farmland, they reached the circling stone walls of Vatican City. Leoni parked the vehicle in the Gran Melia and then they moved, walking along *Via Del Fondamenta* until they finally reached the rectangular brick building with six arched windows. The Sistine Chapel didn't stand out like some gaudy attraction or fairground spectacle. Rather, it stood separate and resolute from the buildings around it, a thing demanding attention in and of itself—a snapshot into a bygone era. The large, archaic structure stretched into the sky, a solid foundation beneath the heavens. Adele couldn't help but find herself staring much in the same way she felt tempted to do with Agent Leoni.

As she strolled slowly under the sunlight toward the chapel doors, feeling the gentle breeze against her cheeks and the warmth on her forehead, she couldn't help but shake a memory.

A memory as a young girl. A memory of coming here before with her mother. It had been after the split. After they had left Germany. Her mother had been afraid that perhaps her daughter wouldn't be given the full experience of family vacations, travel, and life experience. As a single parent, she had done everything to the max, desperately trying to make up for any holes that might've existed in her daughter's life. They had traveled often, using their home in Paris as a launching platform.

Adele remembered the trip to the Sistine Chapel. She remembered an ice cream cone in her hand, the chill liquid dripping down her fingers. She remembered the tour guide, refusing to allow her entry until she washed her hands. She remembered her mother standing up for her, but eventually taking her daughter off into the washroom and clearing the melted ice cream from her fingers. She remembered a gentle kiss on her forehead, and a quick hug, as Adele had felt frustrated, humiliated. Her mother had made her feel protected, warm, though. She didn't remember much of the Sistine Chapel at all from the trip. Strange that. The people, not the locations, stuck out most in her memories.

Now, as she moved with the handsome agent away from the parked car toward the Sistine Chapel, stray, loose pieces of gravel crunched underfoot, and her mind continued to wander back to that fateful day. She couldn't remember exactly what her mother had looked like. Some of the memories were fading; even the beautiful memories ended up swirling, swirling, being dragged into a drain, unable to resist the gravitational pull of an even stronger recollection... Adele shivered now as images flashed.

Fingers sliced, a stitchwork of cuts and torturous marks up and down her mother's body, discarded on the side of a jogging path in the park. *Bleeding, bleeding, always bleeding.*

"Agent Sharp?" said a quiet voice.

She blinked, the searing images disappearing for a moment. Adele glanced over toward where Agent Leoni stood. Once, she had likened John Renee to a James Bond villain. If that were true, then Leoni was like James Bond himself.

Expressionless and stoic for the most part, save a coy smile creeping across his lips as if he found something funny in all things, Leoni wore an immaculate suit, as if he were just stepping out of a dinner party, rather than onto a crime scene. He was, of course, impossibly handsome, with nothing out of place save the single superman curl of hair against his forehead.

He looked at her, the same little smile in the corner of his lips; they curved down for a moment as he studied her. "Are you all right? You look pale. If you need to stop to get some food, I don't mind."

She quickly shook her head, realizing her hand was trembling. She jammed her fingers into her pocket, and said, "I'm fine. Just get a little bit airsick. It's not a big deal."

"Of course not," he said, curtly, looking away to spare her. Then, with careful strides, not quickly so she could keep up without jogging, he moved back toward the chapel, allowing her to gather herself, breathe a few times to clear her mind, and then follow.

She was grateful he was ignoring her for the moment. There was nothing Agent Leoni could offer her except, perhaps, a beautiful distraction from the memories and thoughts swirling through her brain.

Exhaling deeply, she entered through the museum's entrance into the entry hall. The walls were lined with ornamental paintings in golden frames, and the halls were wide, leading toward the deeper portion of the structure and the heart of the chapel itself. Adele looked around, examining the nearest paintings for a moment—some of the frames were wider than she was tall.

No sooner had she entered than she spotted two police officers standing by a small table, with seats that looked to have been dragged in from porch seating. Two men were sitting at the table. One of them in neat, tidy blues, sitting closest to a mop bucket. She took this to be the custodian. The other had a golden name tag, and a twitchy disposition which he leveled on the police officers guarding them. The twitchy one with the golden name tag gnawed on the corner of his lip. He was a middle-aged man, with glasses and silver sideburns.

Adele stepped passed Leoni, approaching the table. "Good morning," she said, softly. "My name is Agent Sharp. Are you Docent Vicente? Do you speak English?"

The man with the glasses looked at her, nervously, and nodded once. The custodian was staring past her. Clearly, Agent Leoni's movie star good looks weren't lost on everyone in the room.

She looked from the custodian to the docent. "I'm sorry for keeping you here for so long. I won't waste any more of your time. Are you the one who found the body?"

The docent hesitated, then nodded once. "I do speak English," he murmured. She supposed he would—given his role in guiding tours from all over. The man leaned back in the chair, eliciting a small, metallic creak from the seat. He sighed toward the cavernous ceiling and folded his trembling fingers in his lap. "I've been waiting for hours."

"Yes, I'm sorry," she said. "This won't take long. So you found the body?"

He cleared his throat and adjusted the golden name tag absentmindedly, but then said, "Yes, Agent Sharp. It was an absolute shock, I can tell you that. I thought I'd found spilled juice." He trembled at this, his face turning a bit pale. "But it wasn't," he said, shaking his head in quick, furtive gestures. His golden name tag flashed, reflecting sunlight through the large windows above the entrance.

"And the body was how you found it?" she said. "Hanging?"

She winced apologetically at the word. The docent also grimaced and looked away, muttering to himself in Italian, before glancing back at her. "Yes," he said. "Hanging. I didn't look long. I didn't want to. I called the police right away."

"I appreciate that," said Adele. "What time did you arrive this morning?"

He shook his head. "Same time as always. On schedule. You can ask Timothe," he said, nodding toward the custodian.

She looked over. "Do you get in at the same time?"

The custodian blinked and glanced between them. Agent Leoni stepped smoothly in, translating the question into Italian.

The custodian replied. Leoni said to Adele, "He says he gets in a little bit earlier. He was just finishing rounds. Says he didn't see anything in the main chapel. They keep lights dim before tourists arrive to preserve the paintings."

Adele nodded. "All right. Can you ask him if he saw anything strange? Anything out of place? Doors left open, security cameras turned off. Anything."

She waited a moment as Leoni communicated the question.

After a moment, and following the custodian's reply, Leoni returned, "Nothing like that. He did say he was a bit distracted, as it's his wife's birthday tomorrow, and he was trying to think of a gift."

"That's sweet," said Adele. "But not helpful. All right, well, I'd like to see the scene. Do you mind recording a few more questions? Just to get out a timeline?"

"Certainly," said Leoni.

Adele nodded in gratitude, then moved away from the table, toward the main doors. As she approached, she found her breathing began to come quick and unsteady. She winced, trying to focus as the familiar tendrils of fear rose in her chest. She breathed slowly, steadying herself—her eyes closed for a moment—and then, gritting her teeth, she stalked toward the crime scene to face the site of the murder.

CHAPTER FIVE

She didn't need to ask to know where the body had been found. She could already see the caution tape stretched around the room, and the red splotch on the ground.

She moved into the main area of the chapel, her feet squeaking on ceramic mosaic tiles, and more memories returned. She winced as she remembered walking with her mother, remembered marveling at the sheer beauty and the artistic nature of the paintings covering the ceiling and the walls. Some of them scary, others hauntingly lovely. She had always loved pictures of the angels. She remembered the way her mother had held her hand, the same hand that had been sticky with ice cream. She remembered the sidelong glances from the tour guide, disapproving looks, especially toward the children in the crowd.

These memories came, and again, the swirling, gravitational pull of an even greater memory swallowed them.

Again, *bleeding, bleeding, always bleeding.* Severed fingers, a stitchwork of cuts and marks.

Adele nearly bit her lip. She pushed aside the thoughts, standing in the heart of the chapel, staring up now. In her mind's eye, she replaced the images of her mother with the images she had seen on the plane. She pulled out her phone, cycling to the folder Robert had sent her. She found the pictures, scanning the crime scene photos, positioning herself so she was in the same angle as the photographer must've been.

By now, of course, the body had been taken. The rope that had been used to hang the victim had also been removed. She saw no marks in the ceiling, her eyes flitting from the arches to the sheer craftsmanship of the structure. A strange, eerie beauty to have housed a murder.

Droplets of blood still spattered the floor; she glanced toward them and looked away. Nothing to see there.

She circled the heart of the chapel, once, twice, moving around. But as she made her way past the small, arching box-frame, along the edge of the wall, and the glowing orange lights, she spotted nothing. What was she hoping to find? A cigarette butt? A thumbprint with arrows pointing to it, saying, *killer here*?

21

Perhaps, simply a distraction. Anything to keep her mind occupied from the images cycling again, and again, and again through her brain.

This time, she couldn't run away. This time, she couldn't run off to Germany, hiding in her father's house to avoid confronting the inevitable. She thought of the copycat murderer, reemerging in Paris. The same MO as her mother's death. Possibly even the same killer. She'd been kicking over the hornet's nest and interviewing the owner of the shop, the factory where the chocolate bars were made. She should've known better. She should've known the killer wouldn't take it sitting down.

She shivered at the thought. Now, though, she had a different case to focus on.

She exited the main area, moving back to where the men were seated.

She approached Leoni and said, "Did you get what you need?"

"Possibly. Did you want to question them further?"

"Did you ask them where they were at the time of the last murder? The one in Notre Dame."

Agent Leoni nodded. "Working." He held up an old-fashioned timecard, pointing it toward her. She took it and scanned it.

"They punched in and out. Supervisor signed off. Our docent was leading a tour, and our other friend here was waiting to clean up once they were finished. They weren't in Notre Dame for the other one."

Adele nodded, feeling a slight flicker of disappointment. Then again, when were cases ever that easy?

"All right. I think we have all we need. I'd like to go see the coroner."

Leoni stepped away from the table, gave a little bow before bidding farewell to the docent and the custodian, and then moved away, allowing Adele to take the lead back to the vehicle.

These murders were strange enough, with the hanging, the posing, the locations, that perhaps if anyone could find an unnoticed clue, it would be the coroner.

**

The corpse on the table in the small, cold, gray room at first glance seemed like any other—Adele had seen her fair share of corpses before. Perhaps this was a testament to the desensitization of her job. Or, perhaps, simply a commentary on the other horrific images still trying to bob to the surface. But as she neared, staring at the body, she felt a chill creep along her spine.

"Cause of death?" she murmured, drawing even closer.

Adele now wore protective gloves and a face mask, which had been required on entry into the coroner's lab. Next to her, Agent Leoni stood, not quite looking at the body, his eyes fixed on the coroner instead.

The woman wore a white coat, and she spoke with a cigarette-stained voice which reminded Adele of Foucault. In broken English, the dark-featured woman said, "You can see around the throat, ligature marks. Fractures in the cervical vertebrae. Death by strangulation."

Adele winced. "And the wound on the head you mentioned?"

The coroner nodded and carefully tipped the victim's head. Adele winced, spotting a bloody wound in the back of his skull.

"Not enough to kill him. Just to knock him unconscious."

Adele stared at the corpse, trying to think of it as the shell of a person. Once upon a time an American cardinal on holiday. He had come to Italy likely to see the sights, to enjoy some time off from the demands of the smock. And now... cold, lifeless... All the time off in the world.

Also, clean. No defensive wounds, no signs he'd even seen his killer. But also, death by strangulation, *not* the blow to the head. Most bodies Adele interacted with showed signs of putting up some defense, or—at the least—of death upon first strike. But this killer was different. Meticulous, cold, careful. He'd knocked the victim unconscious, somehow managing to drag the body—still unconscious—to the noose. Then, without bruising or scraping in any other fashion, he hung them.

Murders couldn't be that clean. Could they?

Adele shivered as she stared at the corpse. This killer... this killer was treating the murders themselves with care and concern, *not* just their presentation.

She thought of the death in Notre Dame. Also a clean kill. No additional bruising, no defensive wounds. No sign whatsoever the victim had seen the killer coming. A completely different victim from the American cardinal—a tourist. Different appearance, different weight, height, different background. No connection at all between the two.

Adele spotted the only other injury on the body: angry, red-crusted puncture wounds along this man's arms where small hooks had been

23

latched through, to pose him where he dangled from the ceiling.

She shivered. They'd asked for her specifically... Had they made a mistake?

"What are you thinking?" Agent Leoni asked, quietly.

Adele glanced at the ever placid countenance of her temporary partner.

"I'm thinking," she said, "that the victim was irrelevant. I don't think the killer cares who he takes, but rather where he takes them."

"The landmarks? With the riddles?"

Adele nodded. "The second riddle, did you see it?"

"Yes," said Leoni. He cleared his throat, then recited from memory: *"The high place of the Great, never the Virgin's fault, met an empire's fate, pillars of nations fall."*

Adele blinked, trying not to show that she was impressed. "Exactly."

"What do you think it means?"

Adele turning pointedly away from the corpse. She tried to focus on Leoni rather than the other images swirling through her brain. "I think," she said, hesitantly, "that our killer is playing games. Something about these locations is important to him."

"Tourist attractions?"

"Maybe. The press is calling him the Monument Killer. But there are other connections between these places as well. For one, they're old. Maybe something to do with history. Also, they're both deeply religious."

"Do you think the killer wants to be caught?"

Adele shook her head. "I don't know. I imagine not. But I think he wants to play his game. He's sending us a message. Not just the riddles but these murders. There's some message hidden here. And it's up to us to find out what that is."

The coroner was no longer standing near them, having moved off to the other side of the room toward the sink.

Adele sighed through her mask, feeling the gloves crinkle against her fingers as she pressed a hand to her thigh. "All right, I've seen what I needed. We have to find out what the connection is between these places."

Leoni nodded, his face creasing in thought. "Well, the cathedral, of course, was the first model of French Gothic architecture under the guidance of Monsieur De Sully, consecrated onto the Virgin Mary." He

24

nodded seriously. "The chapel, on the other hand, came nearly four hundred years later, originally known as the *Capella Magna*. Perhaps the years of consecration are relevant?" He glanced inquisitively at Adele.

Adele stared, blinking owlishly. "Did you just memorize that?"

He stared back and suddenly flushed, coughing into his hand in mild embarrassment. "Er, sorry. I mean… Just a thought. I have a bit of interest in history myself." He waved a dismissive hand. "It's funny the things you remember."

Adele tried not to smile. Handsome, intelligent, and humble. If she wasn't careful, she was going to become completely distracted from the case.

"Where to now?" Leoni asked.

Adele considered this for a moment. "For the killer to subdue the victim, to be able to drag the body into these places, after hours, and know the layout well enough to put a rope around their neck and hang them, then they must have a precise knowledge of the buildings themselves. Which means they've definitely visited before."

"Maybe they found blueprints online?"

Adele shook her head. "Maybe, but if they're this interested in these places, they will have scoped it out."

"You seem quite certain."

"Call it a hunch. Regardless, we ought to track any ledgers, payment information, or guest lists of anyone in common who has visited both places."

"What if they used a fake name?"

"The killer left riddles for fun. Perhaps even if they used a fake name, we'll be allotted a clue."

Leoni nodded.

For a moment, Adele glanced off. She wanted to get out of the coroner's as quickly as possible. She stared at the faucet by the floor-to-ceiling metal coolers. A single drop quavered at the tip of the faucet, seemingly refusing to tumble. She blinked, and realized Leoni had asked her something.

She shook her head, returning her attention to the Italian. "Sorry, what was that?"

He smiled patiently. "I was just saying you seem distracted. Is everything okay?"

Adele thought of her mother. She thought of the images in her

25

mind. She thought of the copycat killer back in France. She thought of Agent Renee, wondering if he was on the case. For a moment, she considered texting him, asking how it was going.

But this would only distract her further. She needed her wits about her; she wanted to solve this one. So she shook her head and said, "It's fine. I'm sure. At least, I hope so. We need to regroup—let's go over guest and employee records. There has to be a connection somewhere—something to clue us in to the identity of this guy."

Adele nodded to herself, feeling another bout of anxiety at the crime scene she'd left in Paris. That was history. This case, though? This was about her future. Her career. Her reputation. All eyes were watching. History would have to wait. The future beckoned.

Besides, if anyone could solve the case of the copycat without her, it would be John. She had to count on him; what other choice did she have?

CHAPTER SIX

Agent John Renee folded the leather wallet around his set of lockpicks. It had been a while since he'd had to use them, especially on the job.

The tall Frenchman stood in the hallway of the apartment building, glancing one way then the other. The neighbors hadn't spotted him. So far, so good. He swallowed, placing the lockpick wallet back in his pocket, then reaching out tentatively toward the door handle.

Sometimes, boundaries were set for a good reason. And in John's estimation, that reason was often an invitation for him to cross it.

The case of the copycat killer was up to him. It had originally been assigned to Agent Paige, but he'd begged, pleaded, and bribed. After nearly three eighteen-hour days of Paige's paperwork, and a series of promises to Foucault he'd be on his best behavior, he'd been assigned the case.

He shivered, remembering the crime scene in the dingy park, beneath the malfunctioning safety light. The young woman had been tortured to death, and such images were hard to dislodge from one's memory. Which was why he was here.

For a moment, John stood on the threshold, holding the handle but not turning it. The metal was cold beneath his fingertips.

Some boundaries couldn't be uncrossed. He knew more about the case than most of the local authorities. Adele had let him in on her own findings.

And yet, the trail was going cold. He hadn't managed to come up with anything new.

"Which is why I'm here," he said, speaking to the door. Perhaps by hearing the words it would ease his conscience to what he was about to do.

He dabbed at a tooth with the tip of his tongue and then pushed open the door, stepping into Adele Sharp's apartment in Paris.

As he did, he quickly closed the door behind him. The moment it clicked shut, he breathed a slow sigh of relief. Invading the apartment of his colleague and friend wouldn't bear up under witness speculation.

Adele had shared with him things she'd known about the case. Things even the locals didn't have. Things that weren't even in the case files. But now, a week had passed since the copycat killer had attacked, and there were no leads. But John wasn't one to be held back by setbacks. If anyone had something hidden away, it would be Adele.

The tall Frenchman scratched at the scar beneath his chin, moving slowly through the apartment. The floorboards creaked beneath his feet, reminding him of the age of the building. One of the older apartment complexes in Paris. There was a neat row of dishes in a dry rack by the sink. He spotted a cereal bowl, yet to be cleaned, resting in one of the basins. Beside the fridge, the microwave, and the oven, the kitchen was relatively sparse, displaying only a single cupboard for dishes.

Adele was often the sort to pack light. It allowed her to move at a moment's notice.

He wrinkled his brow at this thought. Adele was her own woman. She could make up her mind about what she wanted to do with her life. She'd been very clear the last time they'd spoken. She wanted some space.

He moved further into the apartment, glancing at the furniture in the living room just off the kitchen. Also small and sparse. This was not a home for entertaining guests. There wasn't even a TV. He moved down the hall, heading past the bathroom and toward the single bedroom.

The door was slightly ajar, and his hand hovered.

John wasn't familiar with guilt. It wasn't an emotion that cropped up that much in his life. So it took him a moment to realize the source of the needles in his stomach.

If Adele ever found out, she wouldn't be happy. But then again, she had already distanced herself. He had thought things were changing between them. He remembered their kiss, the night spent in the motel after news about Robert. Then again, maybe she had just been emotional.

But he also remembered the time at Robert's swimming pool, the attempted kiss in the parking lot outside the hospital. Then again, if they really were so close, how come he had never been here before? Her apartment wasn't exactly what he had imagined. But it wasn't far. Neat, sparse, lacking most modes of human entertainment or comfort. He had seen soldiers with similar arrays, even after returning from duty. Sometimes training was hard to forget.

John moved into her bedroom, steeling himself. If he was going to

28

do it, he would do it right. Besides, if he managed to find this killer, she'd thank him soon enough.

He moved across toward the bed with a single pillow and a thin blanket. Again, very little comfort. No TV in here either.

He moved over to the desk, noting a thin layer of dust had accumulated across the back. A rectangular portion in the center of the desk, mostly clear of dust, suggested this was where Adele would place her laptop when she worked.

He began scanning the contents of the first drawer.

He tried the second drawer, and it was stuck at first, but as it pulled, it creaked against the wood. A pile of sticky notes, some staples, an old folder which was empty when he glanced inside.

He wrinkled his nose and turned toward the bed, dropping to hands and knees. He grunted as he peered beneath the frame and spotted an empty suitcase. Fitting. A clean sweatband sat on a pair of blue and gray running shoes.

He grunted as he pushed up, moving over to the nightstand. A single lamp, with no shade. And there, a small journal. He lifted the journal and opened it, but it was empty. He frowned, and spotted a couple of places where notes had been torn out.

He placed it back down. As he did, a piece of paper fluttered out of the journal and fell behind the desk.

He frowned, peering at it, but then shook his head. Just a piece of trash.

For a moment, he thought to do her a favor and throw it away, but then decided he ought to leave the thing where he found it unless he wanted to face questions he had no answers for. As he began to place the piece of paper back into the notebook, he paused.

He lifted the thing; not paper. Rather a wrapper. The yellowish-brown wrapper of a Carambar.

Adele had spoken of them before. In fact, he seemed to recollect they had something to do with her mother's killer. Foucault had chewed her out for interviewing factory workers in a chocolate bar packing facility.

He shifted and flipped open the wrapper. There, in marker, were written the words, "I miss her too."

John stared, and then felt a prickle across his spine. This wasn't Adele's handwriting.

I miss her too.

Not trash then. Something important.

The wrapper looked fresh enough. So not something from a decade ago, not something old.

Her father? John highly doubted it. Adele and her father hadn't been on good terms. He wouldn't want to agitate old wounds.

Adele had once mentioned someone taunting her mother with jokes on wrappers. And now this...

He stared at the little wrapper, pulled out his phone, and took a photo of it.

Adele had been on the right trail. He took a picture, and then another, and then placed the strange wrapper back in the notebook and placed it back on the nightstand. After another quick survey of the room, refusing to go through her clothing drawer, deciding that some things were best left unseen, he turned and moved out of the room.

Adele had been on the right trail. But he'd heard what had happened at the crime scene in Paris. He'd heard the quaver in her voice when he'd talked to her. He'd seen that sort of PTSD before. Many times in soldiers. Hell, he'd tasted his own share.

Adele would come back at her own pace. She always did. No one was nearly as relentless. And in the meantime, John would make sure she had something to come back to. Something that would blow the case wide open. Now, he just had to find what that was.

CHAPTER SEVEN

Adele had once heard that Italy had some of the best views in the world. Sitting in the precinct at the Vatican, staring across the break room table where Agent Leoni was running files on his computer, she couldn't help but agree.

A truly breathtaking view. She could get used to this. Adele tried not to smile at the thought, and finally closed her eyes, refocusing.

She'd been impressed Agent Leoni had memorized the riddle so quickly. And now she cycled through it in her own mind.

The high place of the Great
never the Virgin's fault
met an empire's fate
pillars of nations fall

A few points of the riddle stood out in particular. Especially the part about the virgin. This seemed the most specific clue.

What did it mean, though? If she knew the answer, perhaps the clue would be obvious. And how about the portion that mentioned the high point?

A mountain? A skyscraper? Maybe some old tower.

A high point. A virgin. She cycled in her mind through the riddle, her eyes still shut, watching the words spin across her closed gaze.

If she wanted to beat the killer to his next destination, she would have to figure out the clue before he killed again.

She opened her eyes and glanced at Leoni once more.

He gnawed on the corner of his lip, displaying a focus, a concentration she had yet to see. Normally, up to this point, his expressions had been so eased and guarded.

"Any hits?" she asked. As she spoke, she couldn't bring herself to look away from his eyes—dark, deep, contemplative. John was in France. She didn't know what to make of all that. Sometimes distractions were best when packaged in beauty.

"No hits," Leoni said. "But it's not done yet."

"We're looking at guests' details and employees, yes?"

Leoni nodded. "Notre Dame doesn't have an extensive list of guests. But in the gift shop outside we can cross-reference payment info. That's what I'm doing."

"Right, good. And employees?"

"Checking back ten years. Anyone who might be associated with both those locations. Do you have any ideas about the riddle?"

Adele sighed, looking away from Leoni for the first time and glancing at one of the vending machines in the back of the precinct break room.

She nibbled on the corner of her lip. "I can't be sure," she said. "It's not exactly specific enough. It's the sort of thing, I think, that will make sense once we know the location. But until then, it could mean anything. High point? It could be a mountain, it could be a tall building. It might be a metaphor. And this part about the virgin. I'm thinking St. Mary, or maybe someone else."

"Maybe another cathedral?"

"Could be. I can't be sure."

Just then, Agent Leoni's gaze flicked back toward the computer, and his eyebrows flicked up, just briefly.

"Anything?" she asked.

His eyebrows retreated, leaving the strange Superman curl of hair to return to its normal peak.

"One hit," he said.

Adele waited.

"A tour guide, he worked at both locations in the last five years. First Notre Dame, but he left when that big fire closed it down temporarily. Then at the Sistine Chapel. He's been working there since."

"Name?"

"Robert Ager."

"Robert?"

He looked up. "You know the guy?"

"No. Just, I know someone who shares the name. Do we have an address for Mr. Ager?"

Leoni was nodding and Adele pushed aside thoughts of the riddle and got to her feet, moving away from the break room table. She waited for Leoni to join her by the door, and then together, they began to move up the hall of the precinct toward where they'd parked their car.

"Should we bring backup?" Leoni asked.

"No time. If we're on the move, the killer is too."

Adele took the lead, passing Leoni as the two of them hurried with rapid footfalls toward their waiting vehicle.

***

Leoni pulled the vehicle up to the white and beige two-story home behind a brick wall in the Trastevere residential neighborhood. The wind brushed softly against the car, inhibited by the beige and stone buildings, the scatterings of marble water fountains and the old structures looming into the sky.

The doors sprang open as Adele exited the car in a rush, stepping onto the low, street-level sidewalk marked by fading white paint. She looked over. "Did you call ahead?"

Leoni shook his head across the top of the car. "Didn't want to give him a chance to set his alibi."

Adele's hair, miraculously, had become tidier over the intervening hours. Quick glances into the rearview mirror and reflective, tinted windows had given her the opportunity to readjust what normally would require a good half hour in front of the bathroom mirror.

She looked to Agent Leoni as he rounded the car and joined her on the sidewalk. She wasn't used to her partner waiting for her to take the lead. Agent John Renee would often stalk straight up to a suspect's house, indifferent to whether Adele joined him or not. Leoni had a more measured approach.

She wasn't sure why she kept thinking about John. He wasn't here. Adele sighed, moving up the sidewalk, between the open space of the encircling brick wall and up the three slab concrete steps.

Adele raised a hand and tapped against the green wooden door of the two-story home. Across from them, they faced a building that looked like a cross between a chapel and a small-town school. Between the buildings, an ornate fountain was filled with water pattering over the edges of three leveled discs.

A few seconds passed in the remarkable residential district of Rome. Neither of the agents spoke, preferring silence for the moment. Adele kept musing over the riddle in her mind. *High point.* Something about that stood out to her. She had sent a request to the precinct, coupled with contacts in Interpol, to arrange a list of all the highest places in Europe. Any tall tourist attraction.

She had also asked for a list of St. Mary's cathedrals and churches—anything to do with *a virgin.*

She cleared her throat, swallowing back a sudden spurt of embarrassment at an errant thought. She was starting to feel more in common with St. Mary than ever. Something about Leoni in his neat suit, with the soft, fragrant cologne and flawless, movie star good looks, only reminded her of this.

She knocked again, but no answer. Adele crossed her arms and glanced back at Leoni.

"You're sure about the address?"

"I'm sure."

She raised an eyebrow and said, "Want to double-check?"

Leoni didn't sigh in frustration, and he didn't blink. His jaw tightened, just a bit, but then relaxed, and he breathed slowly, patiently, as he fished his phone out of his pocket. Dutifully, he opened to the appropriate file, glanced down, and nodded once. "We're at the right place. Today is his day off."

Adele huffed, pushing a hand through her hair and turning to face the countryside of Bucchianico. Her eyes flicked along the small trees planted in rows across a rustic two-lane road.

"Maybe he's out with friends..."

Before she had finished, though, there was a quiet screech of tires, and then the slamming door of a car. Both she and Leoni glanced toward the street. A small van had pulled up behind where they had parked.

A round man with a double chin and a cheerful disposition was whistling, carrying a paper bag full of groceries. A long loaf of bread extended past a visible gray carton of eggs over the top of the bag. He braced the groceries against his shoulder as he closed the trunk to his vehicle, clicked the automatic locks, and, still whistling, began moving toward the two-story home.

Leoni was already moving forward, stepping in front of the approaching gentleman.

"Excuse me, sir," he said in Italian.

The man lowered his groceries a bit so he could peer over the top of the loaf of bread. He seemed only just now to have noticed the two agents standing outside his building. "Hello," the man said.

This was the extent of Adele's Italian, though. She waited, patiently,

34

as Leoni rattled off a question.

The man replied.

Adele tapped her fingers against her upper thigh, waiting.

Leoni glanced at her. "This is Mr. Ager."

"Can you ask him if he has a moment to talk?"

More Italian. The round, double-chinned man still maintained his cheerful disposition, though he looked speculative now. He said something in Italian which elicited a ratcheted brow from Leoni.

The Italian agent translated for Adele. "He says he expected us to come. Wants to know if this is about the murders."

Adele blinked. She looked at Mr. Ager and decided not to beat around the bush. The man had an intelligent gaze and clearly wasn't disturbed by the appearance of federal agents. By the look of him, and, judging by his words, he was smart enough to put two and two together. Likely, he knew why they were here. "Yes," she said, carefully. "We wanted to talk to you. We know you used to work at the cathedral and recently have been employed at the chapel. Both locations of the murders, which I'm sure you've heard about on the news."

Leoni related her question, and the man's expression didn't change. He just nodded knowingly and then replied.

Leoni cleared his throat. "He says he has an alibi for the night of the most recent murder."

"He doesn't happen to have proof of this alibi, does he?"

Before Leoni could even relay the question, the round tour guide lowered his groceries to the sidewalk and fished out a phone. He held up a finger for a moment, clicked through his phone, and then turned it toward Leoni and Adele.

Adele leaned forward; a second later, she glimpsed a video. The video flashed, displaying what looked to be a small celebration at a local bar. She spotted grainy footage of a birthday cake with the number forty-two on top. She spotted a few other adults with small party hats on and generous drinks in front of them. The camera turned, and it showed Mr. Ager, drinking a beer, laughing and chattering away with one of his friends. A few seconds later, he leaned in and blew out the birthday candles.

Adele looked up again, peering toward the man framed against the two parked vehicles on the low-lying curb. But Mr. Ager tapped at the screen insistently, and she glanced back down, realizing he was pointing out the small, faded gray numbers beneath the video displaying the time and date.

"The night before the murder," Leoni supplied as Adele reached the conclusion herself.

"Is there a way for him to verify how long he was at this party?"

A moment later, before Leoni could ask, as if anticipating this question as well, the round tour guide cycled down, clicking on another video clip. This one showed it from someone else's angle. Mr. Ager smiled sheepishly, as the video showed him passed out, likely drunk, with someone drawing with a sharpie on his upper lip, a small curly mustache. Adele glanced at the man, standing over his groceries, and realized now, that beneath some stubble, there were still the gray remnants of the marker.

Mr. Ager regarded Leoni and said something Adele couldn't understand.

Leoni translated. "He says he was there until two in the morning. Stayed the night with a friend in Casacanditella. He didn't return until early this morning, well after the murder was reported."

Adele glanced from the phone to Mr. Ager, then breathed a long breath.

Of course, it wasn't an airtight alibi. There were still ways he could have worked around the apparent video evidence. And the killer was clever, that much was clear. But more importantly, she knew Mr. Ager couldn't have done it. To be able to string someone up, hanging them from the Sistine Chapel or Notre Dame, it would require a strength, and a physique, that Mr. Ager didn't possess. He was jovial, round, and was already sweating a bit, breathing heavily from hefting groceries three steps. This was not someone who could lug a body by rope. Perhaps he had a partner. But this knowledge, coupled with the alibi, left Adele with a cold sensation in her stomach.

"Can you ask for numbers of his friends who might be able to confirm how long he was with them?"

Leoni nodded and rattled off the question.

Adele didn't wait for a response though, and was already turning, moving back to the waiting car in front of where Mr. Ager had parked his van. High places. Something about the riddle mattered. Eiffel Tower, maybe? The Leaning Tower of Pisa?

She needed to brush up on her geography and history if she wanted to catch this killer—or at least find someone who could help. For a moment, Adele paused by the car, waiting for Leoni to gather the needed phone numbers and then join her. Vaguely, she wondered at the killer. What sort of man would do this? What sort of man would string up tourists and hang them from these locations? How would he have access to these buildings to begin with? Did he break in? Did he hide overnight, waiting for the opportune moment? Did he know something about the locations she didn't?

It was never comfortable thinking like a killer, but if she wanted to catch this man before he murdered again, she would have to.

CHAPTER EIGHT

How decrepit their imaginations…

Rot.

Dross.

They called him the Monument Killer, of all things…. So gaudy, so weak. He was no killer—he was a prophet. Nothing more, nothing less. A messenger, and an omen.

He stepped off the boat, beneath the smokestack, moving in line with the rest of the travelers coming to these shores.

A short trip across the channel. The air smelled of salt, and stale ash from the many cargo ships and passenger vessels that moved through the still waters. And though he walked with them, leaving the boats and meandering toward customs, he didn't consider himself one of the crowd.

His eyes scanned the shore, flicking along the many businesses and shops set up along the wharf. He carried no luggage. Anything he needed he could buy. Just one of the many benefits of a long, successful career as a façade developer.

In more ways than one, perhaps.

He tipped his head, smiling genially as he moved through the spinning kiosk, and headed out onto the street. He flagged down a taxi and stowed into the backseat, rattling off the destination he had in mind.

The driver glanced into the mirror. "Here to see the sights?"

The messenger tried not to let his disgust display across his face. "The sights?" he asked, softly. "I do hope to see. And I hope others see too."

"Well, most tourists choose the Acropolis as their first destination. They tip well too," the driver added.

The prophet smiled again, nodding slowly.

At least the driver knew how to pronounce the Acropolis correctly. So many people failed to honor the greats. Pericles himself had constructed the Acropolis of Athens, the Parthenon itself. Pericles was a prophet too, in his day. A sacrificial leader. The sort sorely lacking in

38

the heart of culture now.

Most people didn't understand. They didn't know the things they were meddling with.

But he did. There were those who couldn't comprehend why these sights were sacred. The home to gods once upon a time, now little more than Disneyland to the many people who wandered through. Sheep trampling across the graves of wolves.

But perhaps the wolves weren't so dead after all. And perhaps the graves had caretakers.

Soon...once he was done, proper respect would be restored.

"Have you been to Greece before?" the taxi driver asked.

The prophet gave a smile. He responded in perfect Greek. Of course, he knew seventeen languages fluently, and another twelve passably. Endless resources, endless intellect, these things were beneficial to most. But to the prophet, endless devotion was the most crucial component. Intellect and resources were simply servants to this devotion.

"I have. It's one of my favorite places."

"Where are you coming from?"

The man smiled, glancing out the window. "Italy."

The taxi driver tried to entice him into further conversation. But the omen-bringer wasn't interested. He was running over the blueprints in his mind. Already, he could picture them. Just another one of the benefits of a photographic memory. He'd worked on such buildings before, called in for cheap restoration projects by money-minded solicitors in bureaucratic uniforms. As an engineer, as a façade developer, he knew the ins and outs of such buildings. He would have to find a place to stay for the night, then a hardware store. He was going to need some hooks and a rope.

CHAPTER NINE

Night had fallen by the time Adele was driven back into the hub of Rome in order to check in to her hotel. Leoni was driving once more, and while he tracked traffic, she'd made the mistake of brushing a finger against the glass of his passenger-side window.

Leoni had cleared his throat. "Er, sorry. Pardon. But you'll leave streaks."

Adele had glanced at him, amused, but then lowered her hand.

She'd already discerned the Italian agent was quite fond of his vehicle, which was immaculate inside and out. In passing, he'd mentioned how the car had been washed just the day before.

Now, as he drove her to through the streets of Italy, toward the hotel that Robert had booked for her, Adele was scrolling through her phone to the newest email Interpol had sent. As she did, her countenance went the same way as the sky above, darkening.

Leoni glanced at her, noting her expression. He didn't ask anything, though, allowing her to introduce her emotions at her own pace.

Adele wasn't entirely sure what to make of the Italian agent. Either he was entirely aloof, or extraordinarily considerate. Given the job they were in, she doubted it was the second. But then again, people had a knack for ascribing virtue to those with angelic features. The halo effect, they called it. And Leoni benefited from it in spades.

Adele couldn't help but sigh, scrolling through the list Interpol had sent. "Six hundred locations," she muttered.

"Excuse me?" he asked, quietly.

She looked at the handsome agent. "Six hundred locations. That's what they came up with for me. I suppose *high point* and *virgin* aren't much to go on." Adele scrolled continually. "Eighteen countries, and six hundred locations. This is hardly very useful."

Her brow creased, and her frown only became more pronounced. Leoni winced. He glanced at her. "Any way of narrowing that down?"

Adele played the riddle in her mind. There were other clues. But without knowing what they hearkened to, it was like taking shots in the night.

She closed her phone, shoving it in her pocket.

"Do you want me to take you straight to the hotel? Or are you hungry?"

It was as he said this that she felt her stomach protest. She realized a moment later that it had been nearly twelve hours since she'd had a bite to eat.

"Know anywhere good?"

Leoni had turned on his right blinker, but at her comment, he turned it off and went straight through the intersection, nodding as he did. "There's a local spot you'll adore, I'm sure."

It was getting late, but Adele was hungry, and the riddle was driving her crazy. Besides, sleep was a luxury. Most nights in the last week, she'd been kept up well into the morning with nightmares flashing across her mind; images of mutilation and torture kept her up well into the early hours of dawn.

She wasn't looking forward to another battle for sleep. Besides, if there was one thing easy on the eyes, it was the agent sitting next to her.

"Whatever you want," she said. "I could eat slugs."

Leoni chuckled. "Is that a French thing?"

She snorted. "It's a joke."

"So was mine," he said, grinning now.

Somehow, impossibly, his smile only made him look more handsome. His cheeks didn't stretch too wide, and his nose didn't rise too high. His eyes didn't even seem to crinkle. She would have to remember to ask him for his moisturizing routine. His teeth were perfect, pearly white.

She found herself staring at the side of his face, but then looked away.

It only took a few minutes for Leoni to pull into the parking lot of a small German café named Sieben Zwergen in the heart of Italy. Adele smiled as he opened the door for her, and she got out, moving beneath the green awning toward the small glass tables in the patio seating.

"It didn't have to be German, you know," she said.

Leoni chuckled as he pulled up a seat, allowing her to sit. "Just my idea of a small joke," he said. "If you don't like the food, you have my word, we can find a McDonald's."

Adele glared at him with mock severity. "You think all Americans like McDonald's?"

Leoni raised an eyebrow. "I think all people of heightened taste like

McDonald's. You strike me as a connoisseur."

Adele rolled her eyes. Now, as Leoni took the seat opposite her, with a casual wave of his hand, he called over the waiter from one of the other tables. The nighttime air was cool, but not cold. The small patio seating stared out on city lights, and the flashing traffic passed the median and sidewalk.

"So how long have you worked for the agency?" Adele asked.

Agent Leoni gestured once more toward the waiter, who nodded and began to move over with two waters. He turned his attention to Adele. "Twelve years," he said. "It's a bit of a family business."

"Your father was an agent too?"

"Mother," he said. "I never knew my father."

Adele winced. "I'm sorry."

"I forgive you."

It took a moment, but then Adele realized he was joking again. She shook her head. "Are all Italians so hard to read?"

"I don't know," he said. "Do you think I'm hard to read?"

"Like a book with glued pages."

He gave a soft, gentle laugh. "What a lovely expression. I'll be sure to use that someday."

"Just don't forget to cite your source."

"I would never dare." Seamlessly moving from a good-natured grin in her direction, he turned his attention to the waiter with the near perfect transition of practiced charm. Adele wondered for a moment at his mother. A legacy of agents. It wasn't so different from her own family.

Thoughts of her mother only troubled her, though, and she closed her eyes for a moment, hoping the chill across her spine would pass.

She looked up and realized the waiter and Leoni were both looking at her.

The tall man in the black and white uniform was smiling quizzically, holding a notepad, and waiting expectantly.

She blinked. "Sorry."

Leoni tapped the menu on the table. "The special is good," he said. "But if you need more time, no worries."

Adele quickly shook her head. "The special is fine," she said, in German.

The waiter beamed at the language and replied in the same, "I'll be right out. Have a good evening."

The two waters now rested on their table.

"So how long have you been an agent?" Leoni asked.

She hesitated. "About twelve years as well. Well, there was a bit of a gap in between, moving from agencies."

"Which agencies?"

"I started with DGSI, then moved to the FBI, and now I'm a liaison with Interpol."

Leoni whistled. "What made you transition?"

Without missing a beat, she said, "Scenery. Have you lived in Italy your whole life?" She glanced across the rest of the patio seating and spotted an older woman and a younger girl sitting at a table, laughing. Ice clinked in their glasses as they sipped from lemonades. Adele felt a soft shiver. The woman looked to be only middle-aged. Perhaps the same age Elise would've been if she hadn't died.

Images flashed across her mind, now, piercing her vision, even though her eyes were still open. She gritted her teeth and blinked, trying to shake the thoughts free.

"Are you all right?" Leoni asked.

She forced a smile. "Fine. Just a headache. I sometimes get migraines."

He studied her for a moment. Again, she was struck by the emotional intelligence of a man who could so seamlessly transition from conversation to ordering food to back again without slipping so much as a smile. He seemed to have a read on her, and she wasn't sure she liked it. He didn't comment though, and looked away, glancing at the menu. "They have desserts too," he said. "My treat."

Adele stared at the menu for a moment, her fingers tapping against the table. For some reason, Leoni's kindness was only making her think of John. He wasn't as polite as Agent Leoni, nor was he as considerate. And yet she still couldn't help but think of him. The tall, scarred agent had been considerate enough to respect her desire for him to leave...

It had felt like the right call at the moment. Some battles were better fought alone... weren't they? Then why did it feel like she was regretting her decision? What could she even do about it? No... she was being silly. She felt like a schoolgirl, playing games. Agent Renee was just doing what she had asked. And yet, for some reason she felt a flash of regret.

She could tell Leoni was still speaking, but she was too distracted to pay attention. She nodded politely, and made the appropriate noises in between sentences to make sure he thought she was listening. Really though, she was debating with herself whether or not she should call John. For a moment, her hand slipped to her pocket. She thought perhaps she could excuse herself, take a walk around the block. Surely Leoni would understand. It wasn't like this was anything except a polite meal between professionals.

But even if she called John, what would she say? Besides, he might bring up the case, and that would only distract her. She knew her place was back in France, catching this killer. But there was another killer on the loose, one that wasn't tied to her mother's death. One she could focus on. One thing at a time.

Her hand slipped away from her phone and folded over her other palm, resting against the plastic placemat.

Once the waiter brought the food, Adele could practically feel her stomach churning. Sleepy, hungry, cranky—not a prodigious start to investigative work. She could only hope the hotel she'd been booked in was more comfortable than the last one she had stayed in with Agent Renee.

But all of that paled in comparison to the case at hand. History in Paris, future in Italy, or wherever the killer decided to strike next. Adele thought to the riddle again, reciting the words in her mind. She couldn't be outsmarted on this one. Not now. Not with so much riding on it. And yet she couldn't shake the feeling that she was rapidly running out of time.

CHAPTER TEN

Darkness fell, but not with a heavy tumble, more like the slow, wafting fall of a feather. Moonlight touched softly against the many pillars and columns. The beige and gray and white stone stretched before the security guard's vision. He flashed his light toward the columns, the flashlight scraping across the marble steps leading up to the Parthenon. The Acropolis, a tourist destination in Athens, and for most a source of awe and wonder at the ancient architecture standing to this day in the heart of the raised ruined city. But to the security officer, it was just another boring job. Paid well enough. No real complaints. Was nice to be able to move around the old stone, getting the blood moving while also making rent. He didn't particularly like people either, and the night shift suited him perfectly.

Case in point, the sounds coming from behind the steps of the Parthenon.

The security guard frowned, moving the flashlight beam and reflecting it off the marble pillars stretching up toward the sky. The archways and the shadows of the protruding stone gave ample hiding spots in darkness, concealed from the moon and the stars. The elevated city ruins overlooked tree cover, lower than the hill's peak. The old stone and scattered rock circled the once-walled top, now wreathed in footprints from tourists and the like.

A cloudless night, and yet, somehow, it seemed darker than usual. A more substantive darkness, as if shadows themselves were concealing things within.

The security guard could hear more voices, giggling. He glared toward the corner of the shadows behind the marble steps.

Other guards would patrol the area, and especially keep an eye on the parking lots and roads leading to the destination. But sometimes people would creep in without being noticed. Others would bike off trail.

It had been done before. A passing favorite of some of the locals was to try to be the first to reach the Parthenon and stick gum to the middle-most pillars.

The security guard was no defender of old buildings. He didn't really care. But he had a job to do.

"Hello?" he called, flashing his light toward the stairs. "I can hear you," he said. "Come out here before I call the police."

He heard more giggling, then a voice whisper sharply, "Now, now, he's getting too close!"

A small, scrawny form burst from behind the alcove beneath the stairs, racing up the steps to the Parthenon.

The security officer flashed his light onto the back of the teenager. A small kid with spiky hair and a single studded earring in his left ear.

The security guard spotted three other teenagers leaning up, peering from behind the steps. He resisted the urge to roll his eyes. "That's far enough," he called out, sharply.

He turned the light up, causing it to shine even brighter. Somehow, this increased level of illumination gave the teenager pause. Spiky hair shifted, and the studded earring glinted as the young boy turned, sheepishly, halfway up the Parthenon steps.

"You can't be here off hours," the guard snapped. The teenager winced, clearly chewing on something. Gum, most likely. The guard pretended he hadn't seen. "You three," he said, "you better scram too."

The teenagers all glanced at each other, then back at him, wincing. They seemed caught halfway between a decision to run away as fast as they could, or to complete whatever mission they'd set out to that night. There was nothing nearly so resolute and determined as a teenager with a dumb idea.

The guard wasn't angry, and sometimes events like this spiced up a normally boring night. But right now he had an audiobook on MP3 he wanted to listen to, and this was distracting.

He said, "You're lucky I'm the one who found you. We have two other guards, and they call the cops. Immediately. No questions asked."

The boy with the spiky hair on the stairs cleared his throat. "Will you call the police?"

The guard shook his head. "Not if you get out of here now. Don't come back."

One of the teenagers was gesturing at his friend, and one of the girls was quickly backing away, trying to tug at the tallest boy's arm.

At last, the boy on the steps reluctantly turned and skimmed back down the steps to join his friends. Once again they laughed and giggled as they ran away, feeling the relief of outpacing any potential pursuer—

then they disappeared into the night, heading toward the exit.

The security guard rolled his eyes. He took a few quick steps after them, allowing the light to bob up and down so they knew he was following.

Then he clicked off the flashlight, more for their sake than his. If they didn't know where he was, maybe they would think he was following them, and see themselves out without him actually having to get the police involved.

Still, he supposed it was best he check. He began to move toward the exit to make sure the kids were actually leaving, but just then, he heard another noise.

For a vague moment, his hand patted at his side pocket. Had he accidentally left his MP3 player on?

The noise sounded like a scraping, a crunching of footsteps. It was coming from *inside* the Parthenon.

He frowned. Had one of the kids already gotten up there?

Feeling silly, he moved toward the steps, taking them one at a time.

His flashlight clicked back on; a low beam this time. The light swept in front of his feet, over the stairs, up and down. He reached the entrance through the marble pillars and stepped forward.

For a moment he didn't see anything, and then he spotted something dangling from the ceiling. His eyes flicked up, and he stared. A rope tied around a pillar drooped toward the ground like a single dew drop. A rope in the shape of a noose.

"Hello?" he said, cautiously.

This was worse than gum. He wasn't even sure how he was going to get that noose down. For a moment, though, the thoughts faded and he paused, staring. There was something ominous about the hangman's noose dangling from the old structure, against the backdrop of starlight and darkness.

He stood for a moment, motionless, and then he heard two wild steps behind him.

He began to turn, but too late.

Pain—a sudden thud. Something crashed into his skull, and he was sent tumbling to the ground with a grunt. He tried to rise, but found a foot in his back, holding him in the dust.

He blinked, dark spots dancing across his vision. He tried to push himself up, but his arms weren't responding. Halfway between consciousness and receding thought, he tried to cry out.

47

But his words were jumbled as if drunk. The blow to the back of his head had been worse than he first thought.

Pain pulsed from his skull.

And then strong arms began dragging him across the ground.

"No," he said, quietly, trying to protest, trying to make himself heard. "Hang on. Wait."

But whoever had him, dragging him by his collar, didn't listen. There was the sound of scraping rope against stone. And then, somehow, the guard watched the noose being lowered above him. He could just barely blink against the darkening vision and the painful spots across his eyes. Then the rope wrapped around his neck.

The security guard tried to scream. But the noose went tight. Still conscious, gasping, fingers scrambling desperately at the ropes. Then he found himself being pulled. A pulley? What a simple, silly thought.

Regardless, the noose went taut, and he was yanked bodily from the ground, his back scraping against one of the marble pillars, his feet kicking desperately, his fingers scrambling.

He tried to protest, but his voice was choked. Now he could barely breathe; the strain on his neck was immense. He desperately scrambled with his fingers against the rope, trying to keep himself aloft. But even his fingers were failing now. The black spots were near complete. Just below him, as he was pulled higher and higher, sliding up the column, noose around his neck, angling toward the night sky, he glimpsed a shadowy form pulling on the rope against the pillar. He glimpsed the old architecture and ancient ruins of the Acropolis. He glimpsed even now, in the distance, above the pillars, the distant city of Athens, the lights glowing orange from the buildings.

And as he continued to be dragged up, his back scraping against the pillar, consciousness faded completely.

CHAPTER ELEVEN

A night of poring over case notes left Adele with little to show for it. Her exhaustion weighed heavy and her eyes felt sore from staring at a blue screen for half the night.

The hotel she'd been booked in, now that John wasn't with her, was immensely better than anything she'd been forced to stay in with Agent Renee. Who, as he often insisted was the case, was booked in rundown, nasty hotels as payback from Executive Foucault for all the headaches Renee caused for the DGSI boss. Adele, in the past, had suffered collateral damage, but no longer!

Yawning, she sat at the table in her small hotel room kitchenette, studying the photos of the posed victims from the last two crime scenes. The hooks in their arms, holding them in poses, were done with precision as well. Did he hang them, lower them again, set the hooks, then hang them again? Was it all done while they were unconscious?

The killer had clearly planned this out, but it was almost... too planned? The plans of a detail-oriented mind.

She stared at the pictures, clicking from one to the other, watching the grotesque images cycle across her screen. Her eyes prickled with a lack of moisture. She blinked a few times, then shook her head, glancing out the window. She winced a bit at the slit of sunlight pouring through the gap just below the curtain.

Out of the side of her eye, she saw the images on the screen, but her mind focused on the window. On the dark room. Her lack of sleep weighed on her, manifesting as a prickle down her spine.

She rubbed at the bridge of her nose, feeling a sudden surge of anxiety prickling through her chest. She resisted the urge to glance back at her computer screen. So many bodies... So much blood.

Bleeding... bleeding... always bleeding...

Adele rubbed at the bridge of her nose, sighing softly. She blinked a few times and felt her shoulders begin to shake. She sat there, shaking, and started to gasp, her chest heaving as she did. For a moment, it felt like bright lights were flashing across her mind. She closed her eyes against a sudden headache.

She continued gasping and closed the lid to her laptop.

She waited, trying her breathing exercises, but they didn't help, she still found it difficult to draw breath. With trembling fingers she drew out her phone, staring at it.

Should she call a hospital?

No. This was just a panic attack. Nothing more.

And yet it felt like the walls were closing in.

Bleeding... bleeding—No!

She forced the thoughts down, angrily scrolling through the numbers on her phone like a drowning victim desperately searching for a lifeline. She ended up in the Rs.

She scrolled slowly through and landed on one name. Robert Henry.

For a moment, she breathed a little easier. She stared at the name of her old mentor, like a moth drawn to light. His name emanated feelings of comfort, of warmth... of homecoming. A better home than she'd ever had.

Almost despite herself, she found herself clicking the call icon, her fingers still trembling, one hand braced across the top of her laptop like someone holding a coffin shut. She waited, listening to the ringing phone, breathing in time with the sound.

For one horrible moment, she thought perhaps he wouldn't pick up.

He did on the second ring.

"Adele?" came Robert's voice, gentle as always. Somehow, even when he spoke her name, it gave her a sense of comfort and safety. Two syllables, yet uttered with such care. He had never called her by her last name.

"Robert?" she said, softly.

"Are you all right, my dear? It's early there, isn't it?"

Adele stared at the sunlight slipping through the bottom of the window. "I'm—I'm... I didn't sleep."

A pause.

"Are you all right, Adele?"

"Christ. You're sick and you're asking me—"

"Are you all right?"

Adele felt the cool surface of her laptop lid beneath her arm and the sunlight bright against her dark-accustomed gaze. She closed her eyes, staving off a headache. "I'll be fine."

"Adele?"

"No, really. I will."

"Dear, it's going to be all right. Do you need me to talk to Foucault? To bring you back? I thought that having something to do might distract you, but if—"

"No," Adele said suddenly, eyes opening at once. She shook her head. "No," she repeated, a bit more quietly this time. "I'll be fine. It'll be fine."

"Adele… you don't need me to remind you. But you're strong. Stronger than you think. Stronger than I think. You can do this, understand? And dear—if you don't solve this case, if it doesn't work out, it doesn't change anything about yourself, understand?"

She shook her head. "Maybe. But on the other hand, if I fail this one—"

"Then you'll succeed at the next. Want to know a little secret?"

"Hmm?"

"With agents like you—no… with *people* like you, there are always more 'career-making' cases. You're too good to be overlooked."

Adele smiled softly at these words, feeling her fingers no longer trembling against her phone.

"All right, Robert. Thanks."

Robert hesitated. There was still a note of concern to his voice as he said, "We can chat for a bit, if you'd like to just talk."

At that moment, there was a knock on her door.

Adele glanced back across the small hotel room. Then, with a sigh, she said, "Actually, you know, I think I've got to go. I'll call soon."

"Are you sure? I miss our chats."

Adele chuckled. "By the fire, in those leather chairs. Hard to beat that."

"Oh my, how time flies."

The knock on the door became a bit more insistent.

"Hey, Robert, I gotta go. Are you doing okay?"

"Adele, I'm stronger than you think, too. Now go—you have a case to solve. And while it's fine if you don't, I think you will."

"That's a lot of faith."

"You're worth it."

The knock on the door was still quiet, still polite, but it echoed out for a third time and Adele called, "Sorry, coming! See you, Robert."

"Talk to you later, Adele."

She hung up and answered the polite, quiet knocking on her hotel room door, exhaustion weighing heavy on her. Now, though, she found the swirling anxiety had faded somewhat, and she breathed a bit easier.

She opened the door to reveal Agent Leoni standing in the hall. He had an egg carton– textured coffee holder, with an espresso in one of the slots, and a Styrofoam cup in his other hand. He took a steaming sip and then placed it back in the holder.

"Good morning, Agent Sharp."

Adele pushed down the final remnants of her anxiety, breathing slowly through her nose. She then frowned suspiciously at Leoni, glancing past him and then toward the cup of coffee.

"Espresso," he said. "Last night you said that's what you wanted."

Adele scratched her chin. "I'm not used to having my partner bring me coffee," she said.

Leoni gave that easy laugh of his. "It wasn't the least bit of a bother. The car is out front." He nudged the coffee holder toward her, waiting expectantly.

She accepted the beverage graciously and then stepped out into the hall, already dressed, ready for the day. She pressed her pocket, making sure her phone was present, and then shut the hotel door, checking the handle to make sure it had locked.

"I'd like to drive this time," Adele said.

"Be my guest."

He walked next to Adele, allowing her to set the pace. Together they moved down the stairs and out the door, to the waiting car. As Adele situated into the driver's seat, she adjusted the mirrors and checked the rearview.

She noted Leoni watching her with an amused expression.

"What?" she said.

He shook his head. "Are you always so jumpy?"

She raised an eyebrow at him.

"You looked like you thought I had a sniper hiding behind me. Is coffee really such a threat?"

Adele chuckled sheepishly at the handsome Italian. "Just used to a different pace is all. You also didn't put up a fight when I asked to drive."

Leoni looked at her, bemused. And she quickly switched track. She cleared her throat as she pulled away from the curb and said, "The Vatican precinct has the list of potential high places, yes?"

"A lot of names on the list."

"Last night, were any crimes committed on the suspected list?"

Leoni checked his phone and looked at her. "Not that I've been made aware of. What's our next step?"

Adele squeezed the steering wheel just a bit too tightly, watching her knuckles turn white against the plastic. "I can't be sure," she said, softly. "It all seems so difficult. The riddles don't make sense. Not unless we know what they're referring to."

"Maybe the riddle is just a red herring," said Leoni.

"Maybe. But the first riddle did lead to the Sistine Chapel."

"In a way, yes," said Leoni. "But only retrospectively, looking back. I think the killer is playing with us. He has all the pieces, and he wants us to play his game. I'm not sure it helps if we agree to."

Adele moved past the slow truck in front of her, whisking away from the vehicle. As she maneuvered on the road alongside the truck, she was reminded of the visit the previous month to the candy factory. There had been trucks there too, kicking up dust, causing her to nearly choke on the polluted air.

The factory had been a lead in the case. A lead she couldn't let go. Adele knew her place was back in France. She knew that spending any more time away from Paris would eventually come back to haunt her. She was tough, strong. Stronger even than she wanted to admit. And yet she didn't feel like it, not now. She found herself picking up speed without even realizing it. She was now swirling through traffic, moving quickly in the direction of the precinct.

"Agent Sharp," said Leoni, quietly, from next to her. "You're going ten over the speed limit."

She jolted, blinking, as if rising from a dazed sleep. She shook her head, breathing softly through her nose, and glanced back at Leoni. "Sorry," she said, quickly.

He smiled at her and gave a friendly little nod. She slowed down, studying Leoni, and said, "If we don't play his game, how do you think we should catch him? You've done this before, so what would you suggest we do?"

Leoni scratched his cheek. "The restoration of the Sistine Chapel was a controversial one," he said, softly.

"What do you mean?"

"I mean, maybe there's more to the locations than face value. Maybe the killer is hiding a needle in a haystack. The other kills might just be a distraction. Maybe only *one* of the victims is the real target."

Adele wrinkled her nose. "The other kills are camouflage, is that what you're saying?"

Leoni shrugged one shoulder, his eyes glued to the speedometer now that Adele had slowed down. He gave a soft, grateful sigh and then looked at her. "Is it true you were nearly killed last year? By a suspect?"

Adele blinked. She hadn't been expecting this. A second later, she felt a flutter of outrage. Not at Leoni, as the question was innocuous enough, but at whoever had spilled the details of the case.

"Who told you that?" she said.

"It was part of the briefing, when I was told I would be your partner."

Adele frowned. "And what did the briefing say?"

Leoni cheeks had turned a tinge of red. He glanced in embarrassment out the window and quickly shook his head. "I'm sorry, I shouldn't have said anything. It's just, well, I had a similar interaction a few years ago."

Adele's mouth felt parched all of a sudden. She'd of course had a number of close calls in recent years with suspects. A number of interactions, often involving Agent Renee. She missed John. She wished she hadn't told him to give her space.

She sighed. Most likely, he was referring to the killer who had tied her father up in his home back in Germany. There was just something about her family that seemed to attract these psychos. Was it her fault? Was it her parents'? Her father was the reason she was now involved in law enforcement. Maybe it had all started with him.

She shivered as she remembered the cold room. She remembered her father tied to his chair, and remembered the killer, threatening her, forcing her to sit on the bed. She remembered her radio, clicked on, providing directions to Agent Renee. And she remembered John, taking a one in a million shot through a glass window and killing the murderer.

But she also remembered something the killer had said. He'd mentioned the Spade Killer. He'd mentioned the man who'd murdered her mother.

He had done so laughing, goading, taunting. Clearly he had enjoyed holding information over Adele's head. At the time, she hadn't known what to make of it. But he'd said something. Something that had stood out. He'd mentioned something about where Adele worked. She wasn't sure if he'd meant Paris, or the DGSI. More and more, Adele was beginning to wonder if the killer who had taken Elise, who had carved her up and left her on the side of a park path, might actually have had ties to law enforcement. It would explain why it was so hard to find her. It would also explain why it was so hard to track down the murderer. They might have connections others wouldn't; authority and power behind the scenes to make things happen that a normal citizen couldn't manage.

She shivered. Now her eyes were glued on the road, fixed through the windshield, occasionally glancing at the water streaks on the inside of the glass.

"It was nothing," she murmured. "A brief interaction. Nothing happened. The killer's dead." She added this last part with a grim resolve.

Leoni shook his head. "Apologies, I shouldn't have said anything. I'm sorry."

But she returned the look. "You don't need to apologize to me." She hesitated. "You said you had a similar experience?"

He hesitated, and was now looking through the window out at the passing tree line. "It's nothing," he replied, hesitantly. "Not a big deal. It's just," he paused, "well, I said it was a few years ago. But it all started before that. It was my father. I was only a child when he left— we weren't close. Someone shot him in a gas station, though. The news reached my desk, and I begged for the case against my boss's better judgment." He gave a soft sigh, shaking his head. He looked at her now. "Honestly, I don't know why I'm telling you this."

Adele studied him, trying to read him. Was this a fake vulnerability? Was it a play of some kind? She knew vulnerability could be a weapon, just as much as it could be an invitation. But Leoni didn't seem cold. He had a warmth about him, an openness, and a kindness. He said, "Well, I eventually found the guy. It took a while. But I tracked him down. Known mob. He had retired from the crime life and was living on some farm."

Leoni shook his head.

"And you confronted him?" Adele said, softly.

"Damn right I confronted him. He had children on that farm, a wife. None of them even knew about his history."

"A serial killer?"

"Old-school mobster. Not much different. They kill just as much, except for money instead of pleasure. It's just as bad as far as I'm concerned."

Adele wasn't sure she agreed. But she allowed Leoni to speak.

"He wouldn't come with me. I had a gun, but I couldn't do it," Leoni said, softly. "He pulled a weapon on me, and I could've put him down, but I didn't. I could see one of his kids, a seven-year-old boy, watching from the door. He reminded me of myself. I didn't want the cycle to continue, so I let the man point a shotgun at my face. He wanted to pull the trigger too. He did. He saw his son as well, but it didn't matter. He pulled the trigger."

Adele stared. "Not to be rude, but your face doesn't look like it has suffered a gunshot."

He chuckled softly. "That's a kind thing to say, I think. But no, the gun jammed. It was a miracle. Maybe karma for what he did to my dad at that gas station."

"So what did you do?" Adele said, staring. "You found the man who killed your parent, then you had him at your mercy. What did you do?"

Agent Leoni shook his head. "I just couldn't get that kid out of my head. He even ran off to get their mother, who was hiding in another room with the rest of the family."

"You let him go, didn't you?"

"No, I did let them go. But I kept him until backup showed up. He's still in prison. Nearly four years later. Serving a life sentence. At the trial, it was crazy how many cases they had against the guy. He'd been on the run for a long time, using fake identities and the sort."

"Killers are killers, no matter what they pretend to be."

Leoni shrugged, nodding, turning to glance out the window again. "Well, anyway," he murmured, quietly, "I know what it's like to nearly die at the hand of a suspect. Especially where loved ones are concerned." He nodded once, glanced at her. "Sometimes it's just nice to know there are others out there…"

He looked away again, returning his gaze through the window.

He was a strange fellow. But Adele was beginning to like him. Even so, she couldn't shake the sensation that if she had a gun pointed at the man who'd killed her mother, witness or not, child within view or otherwise, she would put two bullets right between his eyes, and then another two to the chest, just to make sure.

Maybe that made Leoni a better person than her. But the case with her mother wouldn't end with a prison sentence for the bastard. If anyone ended up behind bars, it would be Adele. She had made her peace with that long ago. After what he'd done to her mother, he deserved the worst there was to offer. And Adele would offer it, again and again and again.

Before Adele could continue this train of thought, she merged into traffic, and her phone began to buzz. At the same time, Agent Leoni's phone began to emit a quiet chirping sound. A bland, professional ring tone. Professional as always. To her surprise, Adele felt a strange, niggling sense in her stomach like she was missing something important.

As the phone rang, Adele allowed it to go to voicemail. Leoni answered his.

He blinked, and then said, "Are you sure?"

Adele waited.

Leoni glanced at her. He said something in Italian. Waited, then, in English, said, "Yes, she's here with me. We'll be there right away. The next flight. Yes sir."

Leoni lowered his phone, looking at Adele where she sat in the driver's seat. "There's been another murder."

Adele stared, her cheeks prickling. "Was it in one of the locations?"

Leoni shook his head. "The Acropolis. In Athens."

Adele gaped at him.

Leoni said, "We need to take the next flight to Greece."

CHAPTER TWELVE

"What do you mean you're not coming in?" barked Executive Foucault's voice on the other end of the phone.

John winced, holding the device away from his face, allowing the Executive's bluster to meet the resolute silence of the dusty window to his leased Cadillac.

Normally, agents weren't encouraged to lease anything besides an unmarked, uncomfortable sedan. John hadn't been allowed to keep the Corvette he'd borrowed last year, but had put his foot down with this new vehicle. Executive Foucault's anger, though, had nothing to do with the car.

"Sir," John said, "I think it's a mistake to try to follow a new lead. Agent Sharp knew what she was onto. She was on the right path. If you would just let me trace back—"

"Agent Renee, if you're wasting time and precious resources, I'll have the full weight of my authority down on the back of your neck like a boot. You're on a short leash."

"Leashes and boots," John said. "I'm not sure I can hold up under the strain."

"Are you under the false assumption that you're funny, Agent Renee?"

John rolled his eyes from where he sat in the car, parked outside the dusty gates. "No, sir. Perish the thought. I promise you this isn't a waste of time. Just trust me."

Renee heard grumbling on the other end. But, at least for the moment, no more yelling. At last, the Executive said, in his worn-out, cigarette-stained voice, "John, don't test me. If you feel like there's a lead, follow it. But you need to keep me apprised at all times. Understand?"

John mimed crossing his heart and said, "Scout's honor."

"What?"

"Just a little joke I learned back in America. Never mind. I'm confident we're following the right path, sir."

Executive Foucault grumbled some more, but then hung up without

58

so much as an adieu.

John gratefully lowered his phone as well. He was being harassed and harried on all sides about his approach to this case. There was a killer in Paris. A copycat? Perhaps. Or maybe the original killer himself. A killer with ties close to the department. One of the killer's sycophants, nearly a year ago, had almost killed one of their own agents. That same agent's mother had been killed by the original murderer nearly ten years ago. The Spade Killer, they had called him. A psychopath known for mutilating and torturing his victims, carving patterns and intricate art into their flesh while leaving them bleeding out around parks in Paris late at night.

The Spade Killer had taken at least four people they knew of, with potential ties to at least three other cases. For the last ten years, though, the killer had vanished. Now, either a copycat, or the killer himself, had reemerged.

John looked through the window, toward the gates outside the chocolate bar packing factory.

He was no slouch as an investigator, but he knew his strengths. Adele was the bloodhound. She was the one who could find a lead from thin air. It was up to him to follow her path. To retrace her steps. He remembered the Executive chewing Adele out for a confrontation at this very facility.

Through the window of the Cadillac, John spotted trucks being loaded on docks, and the large, white vehicles pulling forward, kicking up dust. He had been forced to roll his window up, as one such vehicle had spat up a cloud of dust so large it had threatened to strangle the car.

Now, John fixed his eyes on the man sitting in the guard booth, also watching him.

The guard waved through the window, and John lowered his window again, looking out.

"Your credentials check out, the overseer will see you," the man said.

John flashed a thumbs-up, reached out, and grabbed his ID, placing it back in his wallet. He waited as the guard finagled with something in the glass housing, and then the gates rattled, sliding open on whirring metal wheels.

John pulled his car through the parking lot, found the spot next to an old truck, careful not to chip the vehicle's paint, and then exited the Cadillac, moving toward the office center of the old factory.

A strange place to be looking for a killer. A chocolate bar packing factory. It didn't exactly exude ominous overtones.

But John knew Adele had been onto something. And she was a bloodhound, which meant, as a hunter, he would be best served to follow her lead. She'd stirred up something, kicking a hornet's nest. Had it been from the altercation on the factory floor? Had it been when she'd questioned people at the shop near her apartment?

Agent Renee turned and glanced through the rearview mirror, noting the guard eyeing him.

John made a mental note to keep that man on the list as well. No one could be allowed to skate without closer scrutiny. Everyone was a suspect.

Guilty until proven innocent. That was how he would operate. For Adele, he had to know what else was going to do it. Even Adele herself, the best investigator he'd ever met, had fallen under the pressure of it all. Had escaped to Germany, taking a step back.

He exited the car, striding toward the offices.

He stepped through the doors, and immediately was confronted by a small man with a quivering upper lip and a twitchy nature. The man was standing in front of the door, and on the door was a label which read, *Coordinateur de l'Assemblée Gregor Fontaine*.

"Gate called ahead. DGSI?" Mr. Fontaine asked, his lip still quivering.

John nodded, scratching at the stretch of scar beneath his chin. "Yes, I'm here on a case."

"We had DGSI here before. This time do you promise not to scream at my employees?"

John was reminded of Foucault's confrontation with Adele. He hadn't heard much. "It's actually about that," John said. "Can you tell me what happened? Who, exactly, are you talking about?"

The small man shook his head, frowning. He glanced toward the glass window, which looked out onto the factory floor. John saw old machines and conveyor belts, and employees moving throughout. He saw one man in particular; a pale, bearded fellow, carrying a clipboard. This guy kept glancing nervously toward the glass.

Just another person he would have to add to the list of suspects. Guilty until proven innocent.

John decided the overseer would be on the list too. No one could be overlooked.

"Oh, I don't remember her name," said the overseer. "A loud woman. Obnoxious. Wouldn't obey protocol. Scared some of my employees."

John nodded solemnly. "She is very loud and annoying, I agree."

The overseer looked at him to see if John was joking, but couldn't seem to detect anything. "Well," he said, clearing his throat, his foot still tapping nervously against the tiles, "regardless, I'm not sure what I can tell you."

"Who was she talking to when she had this altercation?" John asked.

The overseer waved his hand through the window. "As luck would have it, it was the operator. Andrew Maldonado. She started yelling at him."

John cleared his throat. "Did she talk to anyone else?"

At this, the overseer hesitated, examining John with a note of suspicion. "She did," he said slowly. "With me and the gate guard. But that was it. She was asking about another employee of ours, but he retired."

"And how many people were on staff the day she was here?"

"Bare bones that day. It was still early, if I remember correctly. A hard experience to forget, mind you." His eyes narrowed again. "The afternoon shift is when we have most employees come in. No sense in everyone here until the machines are running. Regardless, a couple of the truckers, myself, the operator over there, and maybe four other employees."

John counted in his head, including the gate guard. Less than ten. Less than ten people who could have possibly interacted with Adele that day. Ten names wasn't too many. How hard could it be to narrow a list of ten?

John sighed, glancing toward the nervous, twitchy overseer. If Adele was a bloodhound, and could sniff out guilt and deceit, John was more of a battering ram. It didn't much matter to him to figure things out through guile, or cleverness, or paying attention. Rather, he liked to lower his head, barrel forward, and see who was too stupid to get out of the way.

And right now, the overseer was worried. The small man kept glancing at the window to the factory floor, and then back to John.

"I'm going to need you to tell me what you were doing ten years ago."

The overseer blinked.

"I'm serious."

The overseer shook his head, stammered a bit, then said, "I have no clue. How would I know? When?"

"March 2009," said John, without missing a beat. "What were you doing?"

The man spluttered, shaking his head, swallowing, and then spluttering some more. "How should I know?" he said at last. "That's ten years!"

"I know. And I still need you to tell me. Receipts, pictures, family photos, airplane tickets... Anything. You need to give me proof of where you were ten years ago in March."

The man gasped. "When in March?"

John thought back to the case notes. Thought back to the day when Elise Romei was murdered. "The first week," he said. "Give me a broad alibi."

The man seemed ready to protest further. Before he could, though, John said, "You, those truck drivers who were here the same time as the loud agent, and anyone on the factory floor." Then he added, "The gate guard too. All of you need to convince me you were in the clear ten years ago." John nodded once. "In addition, I need you to provide me an alibi for last week. Seven days ago. All of you."

"Last week I was working! Clear of what?" the small man demanded.

"Murder," John said simply. "And if I'm not convinced—if you don't take this seriously, I'll have teams of federal agents uprooting your lives for the *next* decade. Understand?"

The overseer looked ready to roll his eyes, but then paused, studying John's expression to see if he was joking again. John didn't change anything about his countenance—he knew he was as serious as the grave.

At last, the overseer sighed. "I'll see what I can find, and I'll send out a memo. Is that all?"

John shook his head. "I'd like to speak with some of the other factory workers. Get their account of each other and of you..."

"Of me?"

John nodded, patting the small man on the shoulder before turning to the glass partition which led to the factory floor. "Yes," he replied over his shoulder. "To see if they think you're capable of murder. Good day."

Then John moved toward the glass partition separating the entry of the factory from the assembly floor. He spotted the indicated pale fellow with the dark beard stepping around a conveyor belt, a clipboard in his hand. A Mr. Maldonado, according to the overseer. John frowned, mirroring the expression of the overseer behind him, who was studying his every movement, watching as John stepped through the sliding doors.

Was it just his imagination, or was the man with the clipboard trying to hide his face?

"Excuse me," John called out, waving a large hand in the direction of Mr. Maldonado.

But Andrew Maldonado paused on the opposite side of the conveyor belt, glancing shiftily about. For a moment, John thought he might bolt, but he didn't run, and instead, with slow, furtive movements, began to meander toward the back of the factory floor, disappearing behind a large, metal machine.

"Hang on," John called, "Mr. Maldonado, DGSI—I need to speak with you!"

But the man picked up his pace. Not running, still. And now, out of sight, the only indication of his speed was the quick tapping sound of footsteps against the concrete floor.

John frowned, his temper rising as he maneuvered around the conveyor belt as well, ducking beneath the swinging arm of some metal gearbox attached to one of the larger machines.

He hadn't realized how much was equipment was required to pack small candy bars.

He gritted his teeth as he glimpsed Mr. Maldonado disappearing around a floor-to-ceiling set of shelves, laden with Styrofoam boxes and packaged containers. John picked up the pace, his lengthy stride closing the distance between him and the fleeing factory worker. Mr. Maldonado glanced over his shoulder, still seemingly hiding his face with the edge of his clipboard.

"Excuse me!" John called, allowing a growl to creep into his tone. "Stop!"

Another couple of factory workers were glancing in their direction. At last, as John moved around the shelf, he found Mr. Maldonado backed up against a wall, with two shelves on either side. For a moment, Mr. Maldonado reached down, a hand gripping the black handle of a forklift. John's eyes narrowed. He'd seen this sort of desperate look before. For a second, he thought perhaps Mr. Maldonado might try to swivel the forklift around, using it like a battering ram or a defensive weapon. John's own fingers slipped to his hip.

But the pale, bearded fellow squeaked, and then held up his hands. The clipboard jutted toward the gray ceiling above, and in the distance, the whir of the machines and conveyor belts drowned out the first of Mr. Maldonado's words.

John lifted his own hand from his weapon and put it to his ear. "What was that?"

Maldonado raised his voice, breathing heavily. "Why are you chasing me? You're not going to yell at me too, are you?"

John blinked. "Excuse me?"

"You're a fed, yes?" the disgruntled factory worker said, frowning now. His hands were still raised, but they began to dip.

"You seem mighty nervous to talk to me," John said, allowing the growl to return to his voice.

Mr. Maldonado gave a quick shake of his head. "I've had a bad experience talking to you guys. The last time I got yelled at. My hours were reduced. Lost half my pay."

John felt a jolt of sympathy all of a sudden. He winced. But then he steadied himself. Suspects were often good at coming up with stories on the fly. Compassion was all well and good, but it didn't often help to uncover the truth. "That's why you're running?"

The factory worker sniffed, rubbing equally pale fingers against his pallid cheek. "I wasn't running."

"Fine, walking *briskly*," John said, waving a hand toward the shelf they had circled around. He spotted the small, twitchy form of the overseer emerge behind the shelves as well. The small man had another factory worker next to him, this guy nearly twice the size of the overseer. He was also carrying a wrench.

John glared between the two of them. They just stood at the edge of the shelves, watching. Andrew Maldonado growled now, returning John's frown, and muttered, "Great. They're going to think I'm causing trouble again. Can't you guys leave me alone? I haven't done anything."

John shook his head. "Why was my partner yelling at you the last time she was here?"

Andrew Maldonado waved his clipboard, his hands now dropping to his sides once more; they hovered just above his thighs, as if he wasn't sure if he was allowed to lower his hands. But when John made no sound, he relaxed a bit more until the clipboard pressed against his thigh, smoothing the front of his gray work pants.

"I don't know," he said. "She was upset about one of our products. Some old candy. Not even the most popular one."

"Carambars," John said.

Mr. Maldonado nodded. "Exactly. I'm not sure what she was upset about. She just started yelling at me."

John's eyes narrowed.

"I'm telling the truth," Maldonado insisted, whispering, glancing over John's shoulder toward where the overseer and his goon waited, watching. Whether they were here for John's sake or Andrew's, Agent Renee couldn't tell. He knew the blue-collar sorts, especially factory workers. They didn't trust the government. They didn't trust anyone outside. Talking to the feds, about anything, was often considered a cardinal sin. Obviously, this wasn't the place to interview people. He needed to compile that list, but he needed information.

"Look," John said, a little more sympathy creeping into his voice, "I'll get out of your hair. We don't have to talk here."

"We don't have to talk anywhere. I don't know what you want. She was just upset about one of the delivery trucks. I don't even know. She was talking about something ten years ago, but then talking about something as if it were happening last month." The man shrugged helplessly. "I think she thought I was being intentionally stupid."

John tried not to grin at this. He knew Adele had a way of demanding excellence from people who had a difficult time even fastening their pants on the right way. Adele was a bloodhound, determined, a pursuer of excellence. But sometimes, for the average folk, this seemed more like condescension.

John ventured, "Look, the agent you were speaking to has a personal interest in this case. Is there anything you can tell me? Anything at all?"

Maldonado opened his mouth and rubbed his chin, his bushy beard bristling beneath his hand. Before he could reply, though, the overseer called out, "Andrew, your shift is still on. I'm afraid you've spent enough time away. They're waiting for you."

"Coming, sorry, boss!"

He gave an apologetic shrug toward John and muttered, "Look, I can't tell you much," he said, quickly, in a quiet whisper as he stepped around John, moving back toward where the overseer waited. "But after she yelled at me, a lot of people were talking. Like a lot. Everyone in the factory heard about it. But especially the people who were here that day. Everyone seemed to want to know what was happening. Some people had a little bit too much interest. If you know what I mean."

John stared. "I'm not sure I do."

Mr. Maldonado shrugged. "Look, I'm not here to do your job for you. I'm just saying, if you want to get to the bottom of this, you might want to check into the people who were here at the time of that interaction. I don't know anything else."

He brushed past John, his shoulder grazing against the taller, larger man. John frowned as Maldonado retreated back toward where the overseer was waiting. He couldn't get a read on the man. He could tell Andrew was scared. Was that because of John, because of Adele, or because of the overseer, watching them? Mr. Maldonado was still on the list. But so was the overseer, and the security guard.

"Excuse me, sir, yeah, you with the wrench. What's your name?"

At the question, the man glanced toward the overseer, then back at John. The overseer answered, "John," he said.

John raised an eyebrow.

"Does your John have a last name?"

"Smith," said the overseer.

Renee frowned, deciding that whether the name was fake or not, the thug would have to go on the list as well. He couldn't afford to rule anyone out, not yet. Adele had kicked over a hornet's nest and someone had noticed. Someone at this factory. Someone involved in the killing of Adele's mother. And, perhaps, the best way to find a hornet was to keep kicking the nest until it came out to try and sting him.

CHAPTER THIRTEEN

Flashing lights ahead, flashing lights behind. The Greek police had come out in force to escort Adele and Agent Leoni to the crime scene. This, in one sense, left Adele with a feeling of expediency, and she was nothing if not directed in her efforts. But also, it left her with a bad taste in her mouth where she sat in the passenger seat of the squad car, tearing through traffic beneath pulsing blue and red lights in a caravan of police cruisers.

The Greek authorities didn't seem to care *who* was watching, or who knew they were en route to the Parthenon. Which could only mean one thing: the media was already involved.

Adele felt the twisting sensation in her stomach that used to come solely from flying when she was a younger agent, but now hearkened a far more dreadful form of nausea. Eyes were watching. A third body had dropped in the Acropolis. And Adele was now center stage.

This premonition only proved even more accurate as the cruiser pulled sharply outside the barrier of sawhorses against the backdrop of ancient stone architecture at the foot of a rising hill dappled by trees. The Acropolis culminated to the south ruins in the Parthenon. Already, around the sawhorses, Adele spotted more flashing lights, some coming from the scores of reporters gathered around, microphones like swords, pointing out the direction of their invasion toward the old structures.

Some of the lights came from the emergency vehicles parked around the dusty stone, lights buzzing.

Adele felt the butterflies in her stomach twist as she and Agent Leoni beat a hasty exit from their vehicle, clambering out of the front seat and stumbling through the crowds of gawkers and watchers and news folk. They moved between the sawhorses, through a row of police, keeping the crowds at bay.

Adele heard loud shouted questions in languages she didn't understand. Leoni seemed unperturbed by the noise and moved quietly along next to her, eyes set ahead on the Parthenon itself—the purported scene of the crime.

Adele listened as Leoni rattle off something in what sounded like perfect Greek to the patrol officer who had led their escort. She blinked, trying not to let her surprise show. How many languages exactly did this guy know?

Leoni frowned as the Greek policeman replied. After a moment, the handsome Italian glanced back at Adele, moving through the media storm. He waited until they were well past the sawhorses, and the blockade against the public, before whispering, "They had to take the body down."

Adele's expression curdled into a scowl, as she regarded him. She paused for a minute next to the tall, twisting marble columns. Matching his volume, she said, "What? We didn't even get to check the scene."

Leoni winced. He waved a hand toward the Greek officer next to him. "He says the order came from above." Leoni then waved a hand toward the gathered media. "Too many eyes. They had to."

Adele cursed as she followed the Greek officer further into the Parthenon, and came to a halt. The area was cordoned off with crime scene tape. There were already other officers, with evidence bags, combing the scene. Latex gloves and dainty sidesteps did little to assuage her frustration at how many people were already there. She glanced up, and some of her frustration faded to another emotion. A single noose from thick, dark rope dangled from the column above. Two hooked wires angled past the looped rope.

Leoni translated the Greek officer's words. "The body was posed with the hooks as well," he said. "It looked like he was praying, according to the first responders."

Adele didn't answer, shaking her head as she moved around. She glanced to her phone at the file she'd been sent from the preliminary report. As she expected, the same MO. No foreseeable connection to the other victims. Adele glanced around. They were in the Parthenon. A temple to Athena the virgin. *High place* was literally a translation of Acropolis according to Leoni. The riddle seemed so obvious now. She glanced at her partner. "Did they find anything? Another riddle?"

Leoni repeated the question to the officer, and he shook his head. Adele's scowl darkened. This didn't seem to fit with the MO. She began to move around the scene cautiously. Other agents' eyes were combing the ground. She spotted a speckling of crimson beneath the noose, likely caused by the wired hooks used to pose the body.

She shivered as she moved, wondering at the victim. The file had said he was a security guard here. Nothing more. No connections to the other victims. No connections to the other locations.

Just a poor security guard caught on the job. Were these victims of opportunity? Maybe the killer didn't care who he killed. This made things much worse. A killer with a *type* was easier to trap in a corner. A killer who murdered indiscriminately, though... only seemed intent on spectacle.

Even from within the cordoned area, at the heart of the Parthenon, she could hear the shouts and hubbub from the media and gawkers beyond. As Adele maneuvered around the crime scene, she glanced up toward the noose.

No riddle. That didn't make sense. Not unless the killer was calling it quits. But that didn't sit right, either. This killer didn't seem like the sort to back down now. He had a message he was trying to communicate. A temple of Athena, a cathedral, and a chapel. All of them with religious connotation. Perhaps not the same religion. But all of them still hearkening to the faithful. Not only that, but all of them tourist spots. Famous, in separate countries.

"Come on," she murmured to herself. Everyone was still moving around the ground. The body had been taken down, but the noose left up. "It's going to be tucked under the rope," she said.

Leoni had joined her in her quiet circuit of the Parthenon.

"Excuse me?"

"The next riddle, it's going to be tucked under the rope."

Leoni looked at her, but then shrugged. He gestured toward the Greek officer and relayed a series of instructions. Adele and Leoni waited as the officer hurried over toward the noose. A few moments later, a ladder was procured; likely the same ladder used to lower the body. And then she watched as they reoriented the noose and allowed themselves to untie the rope from the column. The moment they did, she spotted a thin sheet of paper fall from where it had been folded multiple times and wedged against the pillar.

Leoni whistled softly. "Good call," he murmured.

Adele felt a small surge of satisfaction, but struggled not to let it display. One of the Greek officers bent over, but just as he was picking up the paper, Adele cleared her throat, her shadow cast across his hand. The officer nodded sheepishly and handed her the note. Adele opened it, revealing typeset writing on yellowish pad paper, and read the next riddle.

Round eyes in round hands,
my longing for you has grown,
Squares in circles once,
My heart is cast in stone

"Anything stand out?" Leoni asked.

Adele read it again. And gritted her teeth. "Round eyes..." she murmured. Everyone had eyes—how did that help? The longing grown? Perhaps a garden? Some forest? Something with growing things? Squares in circles... She frowned again. *Round... circles...* Perhaps the repetition was intentional. Something like castle walls? Or the windows on an old ship, circular in form?

She murmured the last line once more, "*My heart is cast in stone...*" For a moment she paused in thought, rereading the riddle. But then she huffed in frustration. "Nothing," she said. "It's vague. I'm sure we'll know when the next body drops." She folded the paper, tucking it delicately into an evidence bag before taking a photo of the text. She handed this off to the Greek officer and then regarded Leoni once more with a resigned sigh. "If we want to get ahead of this, I don't think it's gonna be in the riddles."

Leoni nodded, and to his credit, didn't try to snag the envelope from her. But once she'd seared the words into her brain, he extended a hand, patiently, and she allowed him to take the riddle and read it as well.

Again, they made a circuit of the Parthenon, glancing toward the teams scouring the crime scene. What were they expecting to find?

No, Adele didn't think the killer would've been so careless to leave behind hair fibers or some personal item. She wasn't convinced this was anything but a smart killer. Perhaps smarter than any she'd faced.

"You know how they say psychopaths tend to have a higher IQ?" she said.

Leoni didn't reply, but nodded to show he was listening.

"This guy seems particularly taken with his smarts. The locations he's picking, the confidence in his murders, the riddles. He's convinced he's smarter than us."

Leoni waited, then said, "Is he?"

Adele grunted. "Probably. I didn't come this far by being the smartest person in the room. Even smart people sleep. That's the perfect time to get them."

Leoni looked a little troubled by this comment, but Adele's mind was whirling as she marched around the Parthenon. She remembered all the tourist spots she'd visited with her parents. She'd come to Greece once before, too. They'd never actually entered the Parthenon. But she'd seen the Acropolis from a distance. She was reminded of her father and mother. And her mother always came with other memories.

Bleeding, bleeding, always bleeding...

She shivered in frustration and pain. She tried to block the memories, the thoughts, but the intrusive notions penetrated her skull with rapid hammer blows. Sharp and chaotic.

Adele paused, exhaling through her nose, trying to catch up with her own mind. And then her phone began to ring. She cursed despite herself at a burbling of overwhelming emotion replaced by jarring distraction.

But then she pulled her phone out and glanced at the name. She felt the prickling of something else. Not frustration. Not grief. And for a moment, even the horrible memories faded. The call was from Ms. Jayne, her coordinator. Interpol.

"Is everything okay?" Leoni asked, studying Adele as she stared at the phone. Adele cleared her throat, softly exhaling a long, shuddering breath.

"I need to take this," she said in resignation. And then she moved away from the Parthenon down the steps, around the building, toward a portion of the ruined city atop the hill which had been cleared of the media. When she was sure she was alone, in the shadow of the Propylaia and out of earshot of anyone, she answered the phone.

CHAPTER FOURTEEN

Adele didn't bother with pleasantries. "Hello?"

The all-too-familiar voice of her Interpol correspondent replied on the other end. "Agent Sharp?"

"Yes, ma'am?" She waited, wincing, preparing for the shoe to fall.

"Are you at the scene in Greece?" said Ms. Jayne.

Adele moved even further away from the Parthenon, toward a dusty, abandoned portion of the Acropolis, away from the crowd, away from the investigators, and away from prying eyes and ears. Her own ears itched, especially the one beneath the phone. She reached up, feeling a thin grit of dust across her forehead. She wrinkled her nose and pressed a hand against her shirt. "Yes," Adele said. "I'm here. We arrived on the hour."

Ms. Jayne spoke, as she always did, her voice crisp, clear, somehow communicating an air of authority and control, even over the long distance. "Adele," said Ms. Jayne. "I don't think I have to tell you that I'm seeing this on television. At least three different countries' news agencies are playing the footage. It's spreading like wildfire on the Internet."

Adele winced, glancing back toward the flashing cameras, the reflection off the glass lenses, the ever evident tirade of jabbering comments and unsolicited questions. She felt a familiar frustration at the media, at spectacle, at a world insistent on participating in every act of the gruesome and grisly. She wasn't sure what made her even more sick. The crime, or the enjoyment disguised as outrage.

"I see the media," Adele said. "They arrived before I could do anything. Not that I'm aware of anything I could do."

"They're calling him the Monument Killer," said Ms. Jayne.

Adele didn't volunteer to comment. She wasn't sure if she'd still have a job if she told Ms. Jayne everything she thought of the media and their monikers.

"Adele, this needs to be brought to heel," Ms. Jayne said, sternly. "I'm putting out fires as best I can. But this is the third murder."

"I'm aware."

"Clearly," Ms. Jayne said, "someone is trying to shut down the tourist industry."

Adele frowned now. She leaned one shoulder against a dusty pillar. Her eyes were now facing the opposite direction from the gathered media. They weren't worth her attention. She stared across the blue skies, visible through the old ruins and ancient buildings. She stood within the shadow of Athena's temple. While she understood Ms. Jayne's conclusion, she didn't share it.

"I think there might be more going on here than meets the eye," Adele said.

"What do you mean?"

"I mean, the tourist angle isn't everything. I don't think the killer is too worried about commerce."

This time it was Ms. Jayne's turn to allow silence to prompt Adele to continue.

Adele cleared her throat. She pushed away from the pillar, and, finding a spring in her step, she began to march purposefully, further away from the gathered crowd and the assembled police officers holding them back. Further away from the crime scene which offered nothing, the body already taken down. Further away from it all.

"I don't believe that he's intentionally undermining tourism, ma'am," Adele said. "That feels too simple, too neat. There's more to it. The most *likely* answer, with psychopaths like this, especially ones who taunt, using riddles," she said, "usually isn't the correct one."

"The first victim," Ms. Jayne's voice chirped out, carrying no emotion whatsoever. "A tourist. The second was an American cardinal on a tourist visit for holiday. The third, now, in Greece, worked as a security guard at a tourist location. I hope you can see why the connection might be apparent."

Adele nodded, even though the supervisor couldn't see her. "I'm aware how it looks, ma'am. And I'm getting to the bottom of it. We already have the next riddle."

"Will that serve us better than last time?"

Adele shrugged again, forgetting she couldn't be seen. "I can't be sure, ma'am. I hope so." Adele reached up, brushing a strand of blonde hair behind one ear. She exhaled, slowly, and stared at the dusty stone around her. "But I don't think the killer is going to be predictable. I think that's what they want us to think. Something else is going on here. Something personal, deeply personal. The crime scenes are

73

religious. But the kills themselves are also filled with symbolism. Why hang them? Why pose them with hooks? Always in some religious pose. One as if they were worshiping the sky, another mourning. This one, from the scene photos I saw, was posed in such a way that it looks like he was praying. It isn't just about tourism. Perhaps that's an angle. Perhaps it's even an inciting motive, but it's not the pure motive. It's not the *why*."

Adele was surprised at how adamantly she spoke, as well as the authority that came as she did. She wasn't sure she believed it, but now, she felt like it was the only thing that made sense.

Ms. Jayne sighed on the other end of the phone, her breath rustling the speaker. "Agent Sharp, I've come this far learning to trust you. And while that's an important component of this position, trust has its limits. One of those limits involves international display. You understand?"

Adele winced. "I understand."

"I'm not sure you do. Three countries are involved in this one. The tourist industry is powerful. Very powerful. Certainly more powerful than the resorts, or campgrounds, or any of the other debacles we've been involved in. You understand? Where money is involved, consequences are heightened. Heads roll."

"Are you saying my head is going to roll, Ms. Jayne?"

The Interpol correspondent didn't hesitate, didn't apologize, didn't soften the blow, but also spoke without any malice whatsoever. It was a simple, professional response, like a banker deciding on a loan. She said, "Perhaps mine first. But if mine, then yours too. This killer is attacking the wallets of nations. More than just gawkers on the TV are paying attention now, Adele. We're talking industries worth billions of dollars. We're talking curators, and bureaucrats far more powerful than either of us would like to interact with. Suffice it to say, if my head rolls, yours may follow."

"I hear you. And I'm on it."

"I certainly hope so. Good luck, good day, Agent Sharp. Solve this one, and quick. And don't be so arrogant to think you are the only one who can know a killer's motive. If it's tourism, investigate that."

Adele cleared her throat. "I will leave no stone unturned, ma'am."

"Good."

Ms. Jayne hung up. And yet, as Adele stood, listening to nothing, she couldn't help but shake off the thin layer of sweat slicking her brow, and the shroud of anxiety pressing against her shoulders. Where money was involved, power was often hiding. Where power was involved, motives were often unclear. This killer was attacking tourist industries. The Sistine Chapel, Notre Dame, and now, the Acropolis. Would the ripple effects of fear cost the countries millions? Billions? Who knew? Whatever the case, fears were rising, lives were on the line. And if Ms. Jayne got in trouble because Adele was too slow to solve this, undoubtedly Adele would be shoved into the same boat, sent into dark waters, and sunk to the bottom of the ocean.

Adele returned to the crime scene, frowning, a lump in her throat.

Leoni watched as she approached, standing in the dusty ruins. "Everything all right?"

"Fine, fine," she murmured, waving a hand beneath her chin. She frowned, thinking of Ms. Jayne's words. Thinking of how this might look to everyone watching if she failed. They'd wanted her by name, but she was sleeping on the job. She needed to solve this one.

"What is it?"

Adele sighed. "We need to go over our notes again. Carefully— meticulously. No shortcuts. As in now... There's nothing more for us here. Let's go."

Leoni nodded, falling into step as Adele turned to march away, past the media frenzy. "All right," he said as they moved, "I know just the place."

CHAPTER FIFTEEN

Another café. Again recommended by Agent Leoni

This time, they were sitting inside, and though a couple of others were on the patio seating, the interior of the small café, which was only a five-minute drive from her hotel, was neat, quaint, smelled of sugar cookies, and, in Adele's assessment, far more importantly, was nearly abandoned.

It wasn't that the business was struggling to find customers, but rather that most of the customers seemed to come in, grab their paper bags rolled at the top, with their initials marked against the order, and then leave beneath the quiet, tinkling bells over the door.

Each time this happened, Adele would shiver. She wasn't sure why, until she remembered Gobert's. The small corner shop her mother used to frequent a decade ago. The same shop where the Carambars had been found. The same shop Adele had investigated.

She shivered as another customer left the café, clutching their brown bag.

In front of her, Adele had a small egg sandwich and a half-sipped cup of espresso.

Agent Leoni sat opposite her in the corner booth, his shoulders pressed against the red and white striped cushion seating. He was staring at his laptop, fingers delicately tapping against the keys.

He frowned as he cycled through the information, reviewing the case. Adele, for her part, had left her laptop back at the hotel. She was cycling through her phone, reviewing the crime scene photos and then moving over to the case files.

They had been sitting in silence for nearly half an hour since the food had arrived. This seemed to suit Leoni just fine. He had the air of a man secure in himself. He didn't seem to need her attention, but neither did he shun it when it was given. Something about the self-security, the self-confidence, manifested in silence only annoyed Adele.

And yet, every time he glanced at her, looking at her with his deep, dark gaze, his perfectly sculpted jaw set beneath his Superman curl, as if he were lost in thought, she found the annoyance melt and give way to something else… a curiosity

Agent Leoni caught her looking a bit too long, a moment later, and glanced up. He quirked an eyebrow at her.

Adele didn't look away, lest it look like she'd been caught in the middle of staring, and instead asked, "What do you think of my theory?"

A moment passed but then he looked back at the laptop. His expression was emotionless, placid, peaceful. He said, softly, "Which theory?"

"The one about the tourist angle?"

Leoni regarded her again. There was something fascinating about his features, and the way the sunlight streaked through the window and caught his eyes, casting half his face with yellow streaks through the glass while burying the rest in shadow. "I think you might be onto something," he said. "Perhaps tourism isn't the only angle. The religious symbology is hard to ignore."

Adele tapped her nose, pointing at Leoni. "Exactly. The riddle this time is as confusing as the previous one."

Leoni pursed his lips, then recited from memory. *"Round eyes in round hands, my longing for you has grown, squares in circles once, my heart is cast in stone."* As far as Adele could tell, he'd only read the riddle once. A photographic memory? She wouldn't have been surprised. Adele mulled over the riddle herself.

"What do you think the round eyes in round hands means?" she said.

Leoni shrugged one shoulder. "Perhaps something to do with the nature of the location itself. A circular pool? A large bay window?"

Adele nibbled her lip. "Maybe a statue?"

Leoni shrugged.

Adele groaned. "It could mean any number of things."

The Italian glanced back at his computer, then his eyes flicked to her phone. "Did you try searching?"

Adele shook her head, but considered this. It wasn't a bad idea. Nowadays, almost everything could be found on the Internet. It was like having an entire library in her pocket. She glanced through the phone, cycling toward the Internet browser. Then, focusing on the riddle in her mind, she picked out the key phrases.

"If you use quotation marks around phrases," said Agent Leoni, "it'll search for the entire phrase, rather than just the words."

Adele nodded as she typed in the first line of the riddle. *"Round eyes in round hands."* She pressed enter and searched the results in the engine. Nothing. She skipped to the next page of the search results, and then the next.

But nothing stood out.

She frowned, focusing, and then picked at the next conspicuous phrasing. A bit more confusing, in her estimation, but important too. The final line of the riddle. *"My heart is cast in stone..."* This time she typed it again, putting the phrase in parentheses. She pressed enter.

As she did, she began to scroll the results, and she found Leoni watching her this time. She glanced up, and this time he was the one to look away quickly.

He stared adamantly at his computer as if he hadn't been watching her and Adele felt a flicker of excitement in her chest; she smiled coyly, but didn't comment. Instead, she glanced away from the handsome agent and returned her attention to the phone's search results.

The first page didn't carry much. The phrase appeared in a few places, though. A couple of search aggregators and generation machines topped the results. But then, on the second page, she paused. Adele tapped her fingers against the phone, and the webpage opened.

"Hello there," Adele said. She frowned, scanning the page. She texted the link to her partner and waited as the Italian agent brought up the website. "See that?" she said.

She waited a moment, as Leoni caught up. Before he replied, she said, "It uses almost the exact phrase. Even with the same punctuation. See, right beneath the picture on the bottom. My heart is cast as stone."

Leoni paused, looking at his computer screen, but then blinked. "It says cast *as* stone. Not *in* stone."

"Semantics," she snorted.

"Maybe." He scratched at his chin. "It is the same phrasing for the most part." They both looked up at each other, eyes locking. "You think this site belongs to our killer?"

Adele returned her attention to the screen. "It's a blog." She scrolled to the bottom, clicking through, and found the *About* tab.

There was no photo, but the section described, in that small portion: *For the true appreciators of culture and critique.*

"A conservationist," she said. "Blog is in English. But he's not native."

"What makes you say that?"

"A couple of the sentences used—too proper, not colloquial. I can't be sure, though. The blogger doesn't say where they're from."

"Well, if they use the same phrase maybe they're the one who wrote the riddle. A conservationist might have all sorts of grief against the tourist industry."

Adele lowered her phone slowly and said, "I'll see what I can find. If we can track down the owner of the blog, maybe we can find our guy. And if not that, at least the next location before our killer strikes again."

***

Darkness now invaded the small café, and glimmering blue light reflected through the open windows, casting shadows across Agent Leoni in even more interesting patterns. Half his face was now illuminated by a glowing blue, intermingled with the buzzing yellow from the traffic lights outside. Agent Leoni had a phone pressed to his cheek, and Adele watched as he talked in his language, speaking quickly, and yet, somehow, even though she couldn't understand the words, still maintaining an air of ease, of calm.

She waited, and Agent Leoni continued to yammer away.

She glanced back toward the café owner, who, for the last two hours, had been eyeing the sign on his front door, which depicted the closing hours. They were already fifteen minutes past. But the store owner didn't have it in him to kick out federal agents.

A couple of times, though, seeing the lights still on in the café, customers had tried to come through, but the store owner had shooed them away, ignoring their pointed looks toward Adele and Leoni sitting in the back.

For her part, Adele would've been happy to leave, barring a lead. Just any lead. One step.

The conservationist had included specific words. The same phrase from the riddle, she'd found also on the blog he'd run. A heart cast in stone... what did that even mean? On the blog, it had simply been referencing the tourist industry. Suggesting the hardheartedness of the museum curators. The blogger hadn't seemed fond of them.

Now, though, as Adele glanced from the owner of the café, and her eyes traced over to Agent Leoni, flicking down his sharp features toward where his hand held the phone, she saw him lower the phone and fix her with a look.

"They were able to track down that blogger."

She swallowed and took a quick sip of water. "How? Phone number?"

Leoni shook his head. "No, from the IP address. The Internet signal."

Adele rolled her eyes. "I know what an IP address is."

Agent Leoni turned one side of his mouth up in a half smile. Again, the shadows moved and rearranged across his face, and the light coming through the window above shifted with the motion. He leaned back in his chair, but the metal and wood seemed to respond with quiet indifference. No creaks, no groaning, no sound at all.

Leoni waited a moment, his phone lowered, and then got another buzz. He lifted the device and answered in Italian. Adele found herself growing impatient from anticipation.

Then Leoni clicked the phone. He began rising. "You were right— not a native English speaker," he said.

"Oh?"

"He's in Albania."

Adele stared.

"It's only one country over."

She found her pulse quickening and didn't blink. "Maybe he killed his victim here, then fled."

Leoni slowly nodded. "It's possible. It's also worth noting, he's at the ruins of Apollonia. They were able to narrow the Internet signal to a Wi-Fi hub on public land."

Adele felt the prickle across the back of her fingers, and she rubbed her knuckles cautiously. "He's in the ruins now?"

"Yes. On a computer. It looks like he's connected to his website; he hasn't moved in the last hour."

Adele glanced up at the darkening skies. The conservationist had used almost the exact same phrase as the riddle on his blog. It wasn't a common phrase. Was the connection that obvious? Not only that, a conservationist of this nature was interested in maintaining old and holy sites. The sort of person who might have a bone to pick with the tourist industry coming through, stomping all over the ancient grounds. The sort of person who might want to make a statement. The sort of person unhinged enough to murder?

There was only one way to find out.

She said, "How long to book a flight?"

"I already looked," Leoni replied. He didn't glance at his phone again, suggesting he'd committed the information to memory. "Already booked. We can be there in three hours if we go now."

Adele cursed. "We'll get there near midnight. Will your agents be able to track him if he moves?"

Her Italian partner flipped a wary eye toward the café owner who was watching them. He said, slowly, "As long as he connects to the Internet, they should be able to. Maybe a hotel, or if he stays late wherever he is right now."

Adele frowned. If they got this one wrong, there would be nothing stopping the killer from striking again somewhere else. Another body would drop, defenseless, helpless... They had to be right.

Adele gritted her teeth. "Let's go. You drive."

Agent Leoni offered her a hand to help her from her seat. She felt his firm, warm hand against her elbow. His fingers didn't have the same calluses as John Renee. Perhaps he wasn't as accustomed to using his trigger finger. Nor was he as accustomed to combat. He had the hands of a thinking man.

She smiled at this characterization. He wasn't as tall as John. But he was ridiculously handsome, and he had a carefulness about him. He was nice. Kind. He seemed to care about her perspective. As if it wasn't just a habitual personality trait, but rather a virtue or core conviction.

She took his hand, and he led her out of her chair. He pushed the chairs back beneath the table, nodded in gratitude at the café owner, and the two of them strode out of the café, moving quickly through the door, out into the darkening night, beneath the buzz of safety lights, and the twinkle of stars inserting themselves over the fog of cloud and light pollution.

The conservationist was one country over, only a few hours away. If he stayed put, this whole headache might be over by bedtime. But what was he doing there? Adele ran the riddle over in her mind again and again. She didn't know enough about the Apollonia to decide if the riddle fit. Was he planning his next murder so soon? Were they going to be late?

For a moment, she considered contacting the local police, asking them to keep an eye on the blogger. To restrain him. But then she decided there was no sense spooking the man. Besides, the killer had only struck after hours. They still had time.

"I need you to break every speed limit there is," she said, sharply.

Agent Leoni nodded as he sidled into the driver's seat, and Adele joined him.

CHAPTER SIXTEEN

The crown jewel of the Apollonia, the monument of Agonothetes, stood as little more than a stone gateway into nothing; the Greek ruins in Albania cut a wistful shape against the black night. Old buildings facing the even older archway of a once impressive structure, now abandoned by walls and ceiling, left resolute as a threshold into the sole unknown.

Night had long since fallen by the time they reached the ancient structure. Adele and Leoni excited their taxi, moving beneath the darkness of night. The destination would have been closed to the public by now. Adele regarded Leoni, who strode next to her, his heels tapping against the sidewalk as they hurried forward past fluttering red flags attached to sentry light posts throughout the area.

"Is he still there?" Adele said.

Leoni glanced at his phone and nodded. "Locals still pinging his location. According to my GPS he's still here."

Adele frowned toward the darkened silhouette of the Apollonia. She ran the riddle over in her mind, trying to make sense of the connections.

Round eyes in round hands... stone...heart... Did it fit? She wasn't sure. On the flight, she'd looked up the old ruins, but had found little of use. It had once housed a school for philosophers... Round eyes in round hands... Did that make sense? Adele huffed in frustration; for now, her focus lingered on stone-gouged steps up to the old ruins.

Adele checked her handcuffs at her belt and then her fingers slid to the holster on her hip, her fingers against the rough metal of her handgun. She glanced over to make sure Leoni had also brought his service weapon.

The blogger, according to Leoni's sources, was from London although born in Germany, and had visited Italy, then come to Albania the previous night. Adele had already been, on the drive over, sifting through his posts. All of them were written around the tourist attractions and monuments in Europe—though some in Africa as well. The blogger, a man by the name of Dr. Francis Boler, had a bone to pick with the "commercialization of ancient wonders." He'd been railing against the industry for nearly three years on his website.

In the night, the place was shadows cast in elongated streaks by the buzzing lights above; Adele and Leoni marched to the crest of the old city, seeing the shadow lumps of the Odeon Theater and the Church of St. Mary. Adele felt her heart flutter a bit as she stepped amidst the old stone ruins, illuminated only by the lights from the heavens, and the second-hand glow from the more civilized fringe of roadway. She moved forward, glancing at Leoni, who kept his eyes fixed on his GPS, both of them intent on arresting Dr. Boler. The same phrase from the riddle had been on his blog—same punctuation. Even killers made mistakes. Adele had yet to meet one who hadn't.

Then, stepping through the stone ruins, reaching the monument, Adele came to a halt, her eyes narrowed.

Her hand still rested on her firearm, and she reached out, tugging Leoni to a slow stop as well.

He glanced at her and flicked up an eyebrow. Sweeping beams from flashlights crisscrossed the sky, spreading through the clouds and flitting down again across the old, dusty ruins. The flashlights emanated from a small gathering of people in front of the oldest arch with ribbed columns.

A single, wire-thin man stood in front of the monument, one step up from the others like a preacher on a podium. He waved his own flashlight wildly about, gesticulating—and, as Adele and Leoni neared, meandering down the trail to the old ruins, she heard the man's voice echoing out into the darkness.

"We come here at night," declared the man with a British accent, waving his light, "to honor Apollo. Some say the name of this city is found in other origins, but the Greeks knew the truth! The sun is gone, the sky is bedded, and the moon peers bright! The sister of Apollo, it is speculated by those who think as I do, would visit this place in the dark, hiding from her brother's ire to pull tricks on his devout. Who recalls her name?"

A hand rose from the small gathering—no more than ten people. The person, like the others, hadn't spotted Adele or Leoni yet. She called out, "Artemis!"

"Yes, good, Ms. Ramona!" declared the skinny speaker. He wore a jacket like a cocoon, seemingly enveloping his thin frame. He continued to wave his light about, sweeping it over his captive audience.

Adele's fingers still traced her firearm, but then moved slowly away as she continued down the path to the old ruins. Leoni slowed next to her as well and, in the dark, sharing only in the lights from behind them up the path and before them sweeping the ruins, they exchanged a puzzled look.

Adele cleared her throat as she approached. She opened her mouth to speak, but before she could, the skinny man in the enormous jacket called, "Mr. Everett, please refrain from littering in the homes of the gods!"

Another one of the spectators sheepishly issued a series of apologies, before bending over with a bobbing light in hand and retrieving what sounded like a crinkling wrapper from between his feet.

Adele, at this point, had heard enough to feel thoroughly confused. No sign of any killing as far as she could see.

"Mr. Boler!" she called out, projecting her voice in the night. "Mr. Francis Boler!"

Her voice boomed over the gathering and lights swished around as one, jarred from their lazy swirl, directing straight toward her. Adele blinked against the glare. "Lower those!" she snapped.

The flashlights dipped hesitantly.

The skinny man in the enormous coat jumped down from his perch near the pillars and stepped through the small throng of ten. In the night he struck a strange figure, like a crow, or a gangly vulture. He stared suspiciously as Adele and Leoni came within reach, stopping to face the small group.

"Dr. Francis Boler," he said.

Leoni shared a look with Adele, and she resisted the urge to roll her eyes.

"*Dr.* Boler," Adele amended. "Is that you?"

He stared at her. "What if it is? We have permission to be here. A nighttime excursion for my students—approved by the authorities."

Adele blinked. She glanced toward the faces behind Mr. Boler. Some of them were young, but they seemed comprised of all ages, and in the fading beam of their lights they blinked out at her. "Students?" she said.

"Yes, students," the wire-thin Dr. Boler said, blinking at her. He had taut features and an Adam's apple twice the usual size. His hair was cut close, silver, and a thin bristle of an attempted mustache streaked his upper lip.

"What school?" Leoni asked.

Dr. Boler glanced over at the other agent. He frowned. "Online. My own," he said. "You can find a link in the *Conservationist Daily*. I'm verified by the journal." He cleared his throat importantly.

"That's your website, yes?" Leoni said.

Some of his suspicion faded as he regarded them. "Are you here for the class? It's online registration only, I'm afraid—though I suppose I could make an exception."

"No, Dr. Boler," Adele said, frowning, unsure what sort of people would sign up for a cross-country field trip online with a stranger. She glanced with renewed suspicion toward the gathered students behind Dr. Boler. "I'm here about your blog. We'd like to ask you some questions," she said.

Dr. Boler stared now. "Questions—who are you?"

"I'm Agent Sharp, this is Agent Leoni. We're working the case of the," she winced as the words were summoned from somewhere near a sense of revulsion, "the Monument Killer."

Dr. Boler's frown deepened across his gaunt and stretched features. He pulled his large coat around his frail form, tightening it as if against a sudden chill. His brow twitched and a couple of the students behind him edged in as if to listen closer. An older woman and man, a couple judging by the intertwining of their fingers, and near intertwining of their dusty dreadlocks, suggested they were unified in their disapproval of all things governmental.

For her part, Adele could feel her stomach sinking. The conservationist stood in his oversized jacket surrounded by a cloud of witnesses. Not exactly the MO of a serial killer. In addition, he was rail thin—frail—again, not the physique of someone who could drag a body up by a noose. Perhaps the group of them, all ten, were in it together?

But even at this thought, Adele realized how farfetched it was.

"What questions exactly?" asked Dr. Boler, his nose twitching, his eyebrows flicking up as he acknowledged the agents before him.

Adele was feeling more and more awkward now. The lights from the flashlights swished across the dusty ruins, the stars witnessed her increasing sense of chagrin. The village above the hills overlooking the Apollonia seemed to regard her with mock severity in the form of glaring orange lights and outlined shadowed structures.

Adele swallowed—she felt silly even saying it, but forced the words. "Where were you last night?"

Dr. Boler frowned. "You're joking," he said.

More of his students drew nearer, shuffling forward, their flashlights swaying. As they approached, Adele spotted more people of a kind. Old T-shirts with peace signs and unshaved armpits and faces—the sorts of people John would give a hard go of. And also, perhaps, the sorts who would sign up for an online cross-country tour of old ruins under the tutelage of an online blogger with a couple of letters before his name.

"That's not an answer," Adele said.

"You're joking," he repeated, his face reddening, the hue apparent even in the bleak light.

"I don't seem to see the humor," Adele replied, curt.

"You think I'm the killer? That's why you're here? Agent, where are you from? Your English is strong. Did you follow me?"

Adele kept her tone calm, trying not to betray her thoughts. "We were in Italy, same as you, and now we're here, same as you. I'd like to ask you about this phrase on your blog..." She cleared her throat, glanced around sheepishly, then rattled off, "...*My heart is cast in stone.*"

The man stared blankly at her. Zero recognition whatsoever. Or, perhaps, an excellent actor. The smarter they were, the harder they were to read. And the killer was definitely intelligent. Evil but smart. Intelligence, though, didn't impress Adele. She'd met many smart killers. People, in her estimation, often valued intelligence far, far too much. Supplanting more valuable things like wisdom, character, integrity, honesty in order to impress rather than aid.

Intelligence was useful only insofar as the person themselves. And as she regarded Dr. Boler, he struck her not as a killer, or a murderer, but a flustered educator with more than his share of quirks.

He was scratching at his chin now, shaking his head. "You followed me from Italy because you think I'm a murderer? Impossible!"

"Do you have an alibi?"

Dr. Boler winced. "For what time?"

"Nighttime," Adele said. "Last night. Where were you—and before you ask, no I'm not joking. My partner and I flew three hours to speak with you."

"You're not going to haul me off, are you? My students need me—I'm the one who has the pass key for the Airbnb we're staying at."

"Are you saying you don't have an alibi?"

Dr. Boler's cheeks went fully red now. And his lips pressed in a thin line. "I can't believe," he murmured, "you'd suspect me of desecrating the Acropolis."

"So you know where the murder took place."

"Everyone does!" snapped Dr. Boler. His cheeks seemed to pale now

"Sir, do you have an alibi?" Adele insisted.

He went quiet, though his mouth hung slightly unhinged. For a moment, it looked like he wanted to speak, but then shook his head and jutted his bony chin out. He glared at her, fuming and frustrated by all accounts, his form illuminated by the flashlights at his back like some sort of perched bat.

Adele sighed and gestured to Leoni, who began to unhook his cuffs from his belt. A few of the students began to protest and Dr. Boler took a tentative step back, but Leoni moved forward swiftly, catching the blogger firmly but gently by the arm. "Hang on, sir. We need to ask you some questions in a more amenable setting."

The cuffs began to move toward the professor's wrists. Before they clicked, though, the woman with the dreadlocks, her fingers intertwined with the man in a similar hairdo, stepped forward and said, "He was with me!"

Adele blinked. Leoni paused. Dr. Boler's lips opened and a puff of breath which bordered on relief but also embarrassment escaped his mouth.

"Come again?" Adele said, allowing her suspicion to show in her voice. "I find that mighty convenient."

But the woman nodded insistently, her fingers still intertwined with the man next to her. "He spent the night with me."

"All night?" Adele asked, carefully.

The woman smirked. "Most of the night, at least."

For a moment, Adele's gaze flicked to the man next to her, trying to put her cynicism on hold for a moment. A normal reaction to such a claim could be read on those adjacent to the lie. But instead of jealousy, the man had a look of embarrassment. Adele's frown of suspicion deepened.

But before she could discredit the claim, the man cleared his throat and muttered, "Me too. The three of us were in the same hotel room in Italy."

Dr. Boler coughed softly and glanced at the ground. A couple of the other students were giggling to each other behind their blogger-professor.

Adele sighed. "Are you saying you three spent the night together?"

One by one, they all nodded sheepishly.

Adele looked at Leoni, who shrugged back at her.

Either the three of them were in cahoots, were lying, or she'd completely missed on this one. She studied their faces, looking from the red tinge on Dr. Boler's cheeks, to the embarrassed hunch of the dreadlocked woman's shoulders and the sheepish grin of the man still intertwining his fingers through the woman's hands.

It was hard to kill a man while in the middle of a threesome, Adele supposed. She glanced around the Apollonia, regarding the ruins, the dust, the shattered ground catching columns of yellow light, and then breathed in frustration.

"I have pictures," the woman added, grinning now.

Adele heaved a sigh, wearily. She shook her head, muttering, "I'll need you to send any," she coughed, "evidence about your alibi to my number." She provided a business card and stepped back as the woman allowed the thing to flutter and drift to the ground.

"Oops," the woman said.

"I'm serious," Adele returned. "Anything to corroborate the alibi. Send it to me, please."

She heard the man mutter something beneath his breath which sounded suspiciously like *pervert*. But she refused to look his direction and instead faced Dr. Boler again. "Stay in town. Which place will you be sleeping at?"

Boler quickly rattled off the address to his Airbnb.

She looked at Dr. Boler, gauging the man. Instead of continuing the same line of questioning, though, she hoped to catch him off guard and said, "What does that phrase mean? About hearts cast in stone?"

Dr. Boler coughed again, refusing to meet anyone's gaze for a moment. His eyes flashed angrily as he looked up at her once more. Anger. Not the reaction of a guilty man. A guilty man would've been relieved at the alibi. Anger was for embarrassment. Anger was for the innocent.

Adele waited as Boler muttered, "It's nothing. Just a turn of phrase. The hardened hearts of the industry. Can't you see it?" he said, some ire rising in his tone once more. "They exchange solemnity for coin! It's appalling!" He frowned, then his eyes narrowed. "Why? Why do you care so much about that phrase?"

Adele hesitated, but just shrugged, shaking her head. "No reason," she muttered.

But the professor was now studying her, his eyebrows twitching. "Did the phrase show up with the murder somehow? That's it, isn't it? Did he cut it into the victim's flesh?" His eyes brightened a bit, taking on a sickly glow. "Did he record it and send it to the police? Truly? He used a phrase from my blog?" The professor was practically beaming now. A second later, though, he seemed to realize the effect his words were having on Adele and he coughed, quickly adding, "Anyone can access my blog. This killer of yours most likely is a fan of mine." He crossed his arms in front of his chest now, where Leoni allowed him his wrist back. He glared at Adele. "Well?" he said. "I have my alibi. Are you going to keep wasting my time?"

She considered this for a moment, mulling over Dr. Boler's words. Much ado about nothing? Perhaps. They'd flown overnight to another country. Shouldn't they at least arrest the man? But again, Adele was struck by the physique of the professor. He couldn't lug a body by rope up a column. Impossible. Were they a team?

That was a theory not founded in evidence. And while she was getting desperate, Adele had never approved of arresting the general public willy-nilly based on theory alone. So what? Let him skate?

If he really did have an alibi... it couldn't have been Dr. Boler. Besides, he was right. Anyone could access his blog. It wasn't like the phrase from the riddle was *so* unique, either. The killer—the real killer—was playing games.

Adele reached a decision, her fingers moving fully away from her sidearm now. She nodded and said, "Send me those pictures. With time stamps. If they don't match, I'm coming back here and I'm bringing all three of you in, understand?" She pointed at the two lovers and Dr. Boler in turn. Then she smiled pleasantly. "Apologies for bothering you. Have a good night." She tugged Leoni and his cuffs away from the professor. Leoni frowned at her, but didn't protest. Instead, he said to Dr. Boler, "We need you to stay put for the next few days, understand? Is there a way we can reach you?"

Dr. Boler nodded and provided his number, which Leoni saved in his phone.

Then, full of chagrin, exhausted to the bone, and frustrated, Adele moved off with Leoni back up the trail, away from the ruins and the gathered array of flashlights.

Adele could feel the gaze of the people behind her burning a hole in her shoulder blades as she stalked away. "Should we stay the night?" Leoni asked.

Adele, though, shook her head firmly. "Not another second here. I'll call the taxi."

Another dead end. But the embalming of time in her job often ended in more than simply a metaphorical corpse.

She could only hope the killer was suffering delays of his own. If not, this setback had just cost another soul.

CHAPTER SEVENTEEN

The prophet drove through the night, observing every speed limit, following every law down to the smallest. An airplane was too easy to track—flights could be followed. He hadn't made it this far by abandoning caution, no—caution was king in this bloody business.

The prophet rolled his fingers, tightening them around the wheel. His eyes flicked up to an old factory behind a sign advertising diet cola. He cared little for the sign, but the factory itself intrigued him. An older construction—perhaps twenty years old. The support beams would have been hauled from a well-known lumber company two towns over. Given his previous job, his previous success, the prophet could regard any building and see its skeleton, its inner workings.

Just another language he'd learned along the way. The language of concrete and steel. But, also, the language of pillars and stained glass. He knew it all, the archaic and contemporary. He knew them well.

As a harbinger—a herald and trumpeting servant, it was on him to remind the world, to remind them all what lay in store for desecration.

And this next one... He smiled, allowing himself the rare expression across his countenance. Once upon a time, he might have cried, even, at the thought. Well, perhaps not. He didn't remember the last time he'd cried. Perhaps thirty years ago? Hard to recall.

But at the very least, he could feel a flutter of excitement at the knowledge of his next stop. The next message.

An important one. Personally important. This one was the oldest of them all, the firstborn of a long forgotten history. No steel beams there. People needed to remember. He enjoyed his task of jarring their memories.

He glanced across to the duffel bag on his floor and, eyes still on the road, leaned over, tucking the knotted rope back out of sight into the bag itself, then zipping it up the rest of the way. He patted the bag and returned his attention to the road, his gaze flicking from building to building, stripping them down in his mind like a lecherous man regarding a cavalcade of flesh. Yet to him, peering beneath the skirts of mortal kind carried nothing in comparison to peering into the hearts of structures—behemoths of age and architecture that told stories for centuries.

He breathed a shuddering sigh of pleasure and, through hooded eyes, watched the scenery, the flitting buildings on either side, ignoring the cars, ignoring the traffic. To him, the people might as well have not existed.

CHAPTER EIGHTEEN

Round eyes in round hands...my longing for you has grown...Squares in circles once...My heart is cast in stone...

Adele rested her forehead against the cool glass facing the street below. The hotel room behind her smelled of soap and steam wafting in from the open door of the bathroom. Her third shower that night. She glanced into the glass of the window, looking down at the reflection of the red, digital clock near the bed. The numbers were just visible in the glass, reversed, and it took her a moment to discern. 3 a.m. On the dot.

Her head shifted again, moving smoothly against the chill window as she peered once more out into the Italian streets. They were just outside of Rome. Buildings had stories to tell too; at least she hoped to convince herself of this. Not all victims could be measured with a pulse. She wondered vaguely, her mind flitting to the previous crime scenes. Old structures boasting columns and art and stained glass windows. Structures across eras, across religions.

The victims themselves were victims of circumstance, she was near certain.

The higher-ups, Ms. Jayne included, seemed to believe tourism was the target. An industry. But this felt too personal. Personal to the killer, to the author of the riddle.

Hearts cast in stone...

She pushed off the glass, wincing for a moment as she turned to face her room. The hotel room was dark and, besides the moistness moving in from the open bathroom door, it seemed as if the air itself wanted to flee her wrath—she felt no breeze, no wind, no air-conditioning.

She wondered at the riddle. The words "round" and "circle" were repeated. Important. But in what way? Hearts cast in stone sounded like statuary, perhaps? Maybe statues of people. The statue of David? Could it be that simple? Unlikely. Uniforms had been sent to the most likely locations. Countries had been called. But it was like trying to find a needle in a stack of needles. She didn't have the key—not yet.

She found her hand curled at her side, half gripping the hem of her old, frayed nighttime T-shirt but also balling into a fist.

Pay attention to your body. Something Robert often said to field ops in training. Pay attention to your body. Your lips lie, your body doesn't.

Why the curled hand then? Frustration? Of course frustration.

She stomped over to the mini-fridge, ripped open the door, casting her legs in a yellow light, and cursed, finding the thing empty. Someone had forgotten to restock the fridge. Damn it.

Not just frustrated though, she thought. Scared. Scared too. The closing of the fingers over the vulnerable palm could be an aggressive tell, but also defensive, like hugging your body or crossing your legs.

She was fearful.

Fearful of what?

The riddle slipped from her mind now, replaced by other images, other thoughts. *Bleeding, bleeding, always bleeding.*

She let out a small, scared hiccup. She wanted to scream as the pictures danced across her vision, darting over her gaze with defiling intent.

She shouldn't be in Italy. Killer be damned.

Her mother's murderer was in Paris. That was where she belonged. She shouldn't have come. Why was she fleeing? Why was she hiding?

She forced her hand to unclench, releasing the hem of her shirt, and, somehow, it almost felt like relinquishing the hand of a parent, letting go of one's security, one's lifeline.

But Adele was no longer a child. Paris was a question for another time. She forced the riddle back into focus, forcing her thoughts away from her mother's crime scene, away from the copycat killer.

She marched to the door, swung it open, and strode down the hall. She reached Leoni's door. He had a fridge too, no doubt.

She knocked firmly.

A few seconds passed.

She knocked, harder this time, for a moment forgetting the little red numbers she'd spotted on that digital clock. Forgetting everything that supposedly mattered.

Halfway through a third attempt at knocking, the door cracked open.

She blinked—Agent Leoni was dressed in his suit. Had he slept in it? No—not a wrinkle. His eyes were a bit baggy as she stared at him and she saw his laptop open on a small circular table by the kitchenette in his room.

She winced. "Hey," she said.

"Agent Sharp?" He dipped his head politely.

"Working?" she asked.

He smiled, an expression that didn't seem forced. Ever the polite professional. Staying up into all hours, by the looks of things.

He glanced over his shoulder toward the computer and nodded once. "Trying to learn what I can about the locations—connecting points. Did you know the Apollonia was once called Gylax?"

"No," she said.

"Can I help you?" he asked.

"You should sleep."

"Thank you for your concern. I'll get to it."

Adele looked away from his open computer toward his mini-fridge. "Is your…" She cleared her throat. "Is your fridge stocked?"

Suddenly, she felt a flush of embarrassment as the reality of her situation dawned on her. She'd come to her fellow agent's room, in the middle of the night no less, on a quest to raid his overpriced stores of alcohol.

Leoni blinked, then smiled. "Minus one particularly bitter gin, yes. Would you like to share?"

"Please," said Adele.

Leoni stepped aside, ushering her in, and Adele moved over to the fridge. She swung it open, scanned the stocked contents, and snared one of the miniature clear bottles. She noticed now, just out of sight behind his computer, Leoni had a similar bottle already opened and half empty.

Adele felt the cool glass beneath her fingers, as she plucked a bottle from the crisscrossing wire shelf and placed it in her pocket. She glanced toward Leoni and nodded in gratitude, but, for the moment, left the fridge door open.

Leoni was an investigator for a reason. He seemed to read her mind, and chuckled as he moved back over toward his computer. "Help yourself to as much as you want," he said.

"I'll pay you back," she said.

"Don't be silly."

Adele grabbed another couple of bottles, listening as they clinked where she slid them into her pocket. At last, she closed the fridge door and moved past Leoni in his chair, looking over his shoulder to where he was scrolling through information about the Sistine Chapel.

The writing was dense, and the sentences long. After a couple of paragraphs, Adele found that her head hurt.

Leoni, though, seemed to consume the information without trouble. His eyes were baggy, and yet he attentively stared at the screen, reading and rereading sections. Perhaps even committing them to memory, if prior experience was anything to go by.

"Thanks," Adele murmured.

"Stay if you like," Leoni said. "I'll be up for a bit longer anyway."

For a moment, Adele felt a flutter of anticipation. She chided herself inwardly, though. Leoni clearly didn't mean anything sensual. He was just trying to be a good partner. Then again, she'd proven to herself she was bad at reading men. John was the obvious example. Still, she had come for a different type of companionship.

She bid farewell to Leoni and then took her pilfered bottles and moved away, back out the door, shutting it behind her and heading to her room.

Adele downed the first bottle in a matter of seconds, feeling the bitter taste and wincing against the sudden cold against her tongue and lips. She moved into the bathroom of her own room again and sat on the edge of the bathtub, the smooth porcelain pressing against her thighs.

She blinked a couple of times, looking at the fogged mirror and the tracing of a smiley face she had drawn on it earlier.

She could still feel her lips tingling and throat burning as she crossed her arms over her legs, listening to the bottles in her pocket tinkle again. Maybe she was making a mistake by staying here. Maybe she needed to go back to find her mother's killer. To be with John. He would need all the help he could get. He was an excellent agent, but he wasn't a bloodhound. He was a hammer, and every perceived problem a nail. Not that it hadn't worked for him so far, but a hammer could smash things that were best left intact. Adele took out the second bottle, and didn't realize by the time this one emptied as well. No sooner had the second emptied than the third bottle emerged.

She spun it around, looking at it. For a moment, she considered downing it in one big gulp. She placed it on the edge of the sink across from her. By now, through her sweatpants, she could feel the moisture from the rim of the tub.

"Third time's the charm," she murmured, examining the bottle.

Except, in this case, the third time was the same as the first two. Bodies in a morgue. And Adele struggling to keep up.

She was supposed to be good at her job. It was what they paid her for.

Adele felt her head throbbing all of a sudden. A steady pulsing ache. She felt confused and disoriented, and slid into the tub, angling so she was leaning back and resting her head against the porcelain slant. She could feel the moisture pressing around her now. She could feel her T-shirt sticky against her, her sweatpants sodden.

She closed her eyes, inhaling the last vestiges of steam from the third shower she'd taken.

Three showers. Three a.m. Three bottles. Three bodies.

Three chances to catch a killer, and three misses.

The fourth was coming. She could feel it. It was coming. And if she didn't catch the killer this time, then perhaps she never would.

CHAPTER NINETEEN

Adele blinked and found her eyelids scraping against her eyes like rough sandpaper. She winced, listening to the slow squawk of the alarm from her phone set on the bathroom sink. The first glimmers of light strayed through the open doorway of the bathroom.

She was still in the bathtub, her clothing still damp, her head pressed against cold, hard porcelain. For a moment, she considered turning off the alarm and going back to sleep. But that wasn't who she was. And even now, running from her problems in France, trying to hide from three bodies with three bottles, she wasn't about to change. Old habits die hard.

She sat up in the bathtub, groaning, slapping her bare feet against the cool floor. She clicked off the alarm, pocketed her phone, and rubbed the sleep from her eyes.

She glanced at the phone. No missed calls or notifications.

Save one.

Leoni had texted her.

Three words. Always three, it seemed.

I found something.

The text had come an hour ago. Groaning to herself, she got to her feet. No calls meant no more bodies. The killer hadn't struck again. Maybe the next location was further away than the first three.

She hastily threw on a new change of clothes and sweater, deciding to skip the usual morning shower. She could feel the effects of the third bottle, and the stale, sour feeling in the back of her throat. Groaning to herself, she pushed open the door and moved, half limping, as if she were dragging sleep behind her, toward Leoni's room.

She began to knock on the door, but as she did, it swung inward, opening on well-greased hinges. She blinked and stepped into the room. Leoni was sitting in a wooden chair, snoring, his face planted against the wooden table. His computer was open in front of him, but the screen had darkened, suggesting it had also gone to sleep.

Leoni was still wearing his suit; it looked like his bed hadn't even been slept in. Sheer exhaustion seemed to have taken its toll. She

99

cleared her throat, but when this aroused no reaction, she moved over and tapped Leoni on the shoulder.

He jerked up and glanced at her, blinking wildly. It took him a moment to catch his bearings, exhausted and sleep deprived as he was. But she'd known Leoni was quick, and his processor took only a couple of seconds to boot up before he recognized her, then murmured a greeting, flicked his eyes toward the half ajar door, and to his computer.

"You said you found something," she said.

"Good morning."

"Good morning. What did you find?"

Leoni tapped his computer. He didn't say anything, rubbing at his eyes, glancing toward the drapes pulled across his window. Then, when the screen lit up, he twisted it, turning it toward her.

Adele lowered, frowning at the screen. "What am I looking at?"

"Website," Leoni said.

"Not the conservationist again? I got his *evidence* from the night before. Didn't know someone could be that flexible at his age."

"No, not the conservationist. I found the site by cross-referencing the different murder locations. Stumbled on it by sheer accident."

"What is it?" Adele asked.

The top of the webpage was an old picture of ruins, with the heading reading, "Bestselling guidebook *Days Away*, available now!"

Adele blinked but shook her head. "What?"

"It's a popular tourist guidebook," said Leoni. "The website belongs to the author. An Adrian Von Ziegler. He's a fanatic."

Adele blinked. "What sort of fanatic?"

"Read for yourself," Leoni said. "Sistine Chapel, Notre Dame, the Acropolis," he said, "they're all there. All of them have been researched, visited, and photographed by Mr. Von Ziegler for his book. The researcher had intimate knowledge of the buildings, pictures of our crime scenes, and, more damning, look at the most recent post. An update."

Adele leaned in, reading the update. She scanned the paragraphs, taking in the text, and then stared.

One section read, "...*the most recent killing, at the Parthenon, is a sign. Not a sign from the divines, but a sign from humanity itself. We're beginning to eat our own. Desecration leads to desecration. The same sorts that would use money-lending tables, overturned once upon a time, are now being struck again. Tourists, flash photography, hot dog condiments dripping on the ground of ancient landmarks beg for a response from the noble few. The victims are deserving. The judgment isn't pleasant, but once the purging is complete, perhaps people will finally respect these monuments as they ought."*

Adele whistled softly as she continued to read the post. "This is a guidebook?"

"It's the author's website. He published a guidebook for tourists. But it's a different slant—full of a sort of awe and reverence for these locations."

"Holier than thou tourists," Adele said. "Great. Is there anything else about the other murders?"

Leoni tapped over to another page, nodding as he did. "More of the same. Complimenting the killer, or at least coming close. Not quite saying they deserved their deaths, but not standing up for the victims either. Hinting and implying they got what was coming to them. Hinting and implying that whoever the killer is, they're fulfilling some twisted justice."

Adele whistled, shaking her head.

"Maybe the tourist angle is right," said Leoni. He looked up at her now, and she could see his bloodshot eyes from his lack of sleep.

"You look horrible," she said.

"And you look lovely as always."

"You should really get some rest."

"Can't," Leoni said, closing the screen and clicking the laptop shut.

"Can't?"

"Our flight is already booked. Tracked the owner of the website. Mr. Von Ziegler himself."

"Yeah, where's he out of?"

"Austria. Our flight leaves within the hour. Ready to go?"

"Hang on, Austria?"

"Yes. Ready?"

Adele sighed. And she had thought she was unstoppable when she caught a scent. Also, Leoni was no use to her half asleep. "I'm fine," she said. "How about you?"

He waved away the worry. "Me too. Did you enjoy those drinks last night?"

Adele gave a chagrined sigh. "I may have overdone it a little."

Leoni patted her on the hand, and then she noticed his bag was

101

already on the bed, packed. "I'm good to go," he said. "I'll be waiting at the curb. Do you need help with anything?"

Adele shook her head and said, "Maybe you're right about the tourist angle." She gestured toward the computer. "Certainly damning comments from someone who has interior photographs of the locations. Doesn't seem at all broken up about the deaths of the tourists."

"But? You're speaking like there's a but."

"I still don't think tourism is the right angle."

"You don't want to at least check it out?"

Adele paused for a moment, considering the flight, feeling like she was being tugged around like a puppy with a collar. Then again, no bodies had dropped in the night. No further deaths. Which meant the killer would inevitably strike now. He was on a rampage, and he wouldn't stop. Especially given the new riddle.

If they were wrong this time, there would be no third chances. And this game was counted in corpses.

Adele felt a bit of her usual fire return, and she gritted her teeth, turning and marching back toward the slightly open door. "I'll meet you in the parking lot. I get the window seat on the plane."

"Done!" he called after her.

Adele hurried over to her room, tapping her hands against her thigh, and wondering if perhaps she should keep Ms. Jayne apprised. The Interpol correspondent had been clear about tracking the tourist angle even though Adele had felt this was a mistake.

Were her instincts off? She felt something else was going on here. But maybe her gut wasn't serving her as well as it used to. Maybe the cowardice of running from Paris, hiding in Germany, fleeing her obligations was finally catching up with her.

She hated the thought, but maybe she'd abandoned her position.

Adele packed what items she had brought with these troubling thoughts leeching into her mind.

Whatever the case, this Austrian author had means and motive, and it was up to her to find out if he also had opportunity.

Killers were all the same after all. Just different degrees of selfish narcissists. Different degrees of cold-hearted and often broken malevolence.

She felt her phone buzz and glanced down. Another message. This one from John Renee. She felt her pulse skip. For a moment, she stared at the text. But then, fingers trembling, she clicked the screen dark without reading the message, and stowed her phone in her pocket. The message would have to wait. The killer in Paris was John's job. Adele had her own killer to catch. And by the looks of things, he was hiding in Austria. Just a short plane flight away.

CHAPTER TWENTY

The airplane was nearly empty this time, and Adele could hear her own thoughts whirring in her mind. Did it make sense the killer would be in Austria now? The website had damming evidence. As she sat in first-class, her elbow jutting toward where Leoni was scanning his laptop screen again, she also flicked through her phone to the stored webpage. The author of the guidebook, *Days Away*, clearly had no love lost for the murder victims.

The air-conditioning was turned off above her. The small service light was also dim. She breathed a soft sigh in the nearly empty plane, grateful for the momentary respite to catch her breath. The flight to Austria wouldn't take long, but Adele knew she needed to focus. The rantings of a crazed author against tourists was one thing, but the riddle seemed another piece of writing altogether. It wasn't that authors couldn't also pen riddles.

But there was something measured to the riddle. Something playful, even taunting. Something shouting *Catch me if you can!*

Could she?

Adele closed her eyes, feeling the sandpaper sensation again from earlier, wishing she'd drunk a little less the night before. As she did, leaning back, trying to get comfortable, she realized she was asking the wrong question. It wasn't a matter of *could*. Her ability wasn't in question.

But sometimes, even the most able ships passed in the night. It didn't matter the guns, the sails, the reinforced hull—if a ship missed its target in the mist, then no manner of upgrades or preparation or even skill would matter.

In order to catch a murderer, Adele had to find him first. She was getting closer... she could feel it. But would their paths cross? Would Mr. Von Ziegler even be home? Or was he out now, while the agents hunting him returned to his home instead of solving his riddle? What if Mr. Von Ziegler was already stalking his next victim?

Adele kept her eyes closed, shivering at the thought. She needed to sleep, but, more importantly, she needed to solve this. She brought back to mind the words in the newest riddle, mulling them over and allowing them to cycle, one after the other, leaving no stone unturned.

...My heart is cast in stone.

Stone. The most important word at the end of the sentence. Stone. She had it... she knew she was close... It was a word on the tip of her tongue, but she couldn't quite find it. It remained out of reach, even as she rested on the plane, her body limp in the seat, but her mind abuzz.

*****

It seemed fitting to Adele that an unstable travel expert in Austria lived in a tree house.

"You're joking," Leoni said, his neck craned back as he peered up at the structure built across two thick oaks.

Adele shook her head. "This is the address."

She glanced along the trail they'd come down in the local police cruiser that had been sent to pick them up from the Vienna International Airport. In the distance, against a backdrop of low mountains, the air was pristine and clear. Adele could feel it cool as she inhaled the fresh breeze.

The muddy trail behind them, where the Austrian officer awaited their return in the car, was mostly obscured by overgrowth, with patches of grass threatening to strangle it. No other vehicles as far as Adele could see. But the house—what looked to be a trailer home hoisted in the branches—had no visible approach.

She craned her neck back, feeling the eyes of the Austrian policeman peering out at her from his vehicle. One country to the next, moving around Europe like a child playing hopscotch. Adele was beginning to resent the killer on the move.

But over the flight, between salted peanuts, she'd managed to read more of the travel guidebook author's posts. More railing against tourists, more thinly veiled support for the killer. If anyone had a bone to pick in the way Ms. Jayne and the other agencies suspected, it was this man.

"Mr. Von Ziegler!" she called, raising her voice. "Interpol—are you home!"

The guidebook was written in English, as were the ranting web posts—at least she wouldn't need a translator this time. The elevated house between the trees, though, remained quiet. No movement, no lights. She glanced around, looking for a home at a more accessible level. But this was it—the only visible domicile.

Adele stared up at the treehouse, studying any way she might ascend. After a few minutes of examining the structure, her eyes slipped along the metal siding and glass windows, and she spotted a rope ladder curled up and coiled at the top of the suspended wooden platform which held the trailer.

She nudged Leoni and pointed.

"Ladder is raised. Means he's up there," Leoni said, softly.

Adele tapped her nose. She could feel the eyes of the Austrian officer behind them, still fixated on the agents. They had arranged for a cleared interrogation room back at the local precinct, but first, they needed to catch their suspect.

"Mr. Von Ziegler," she called, her voice rising toward the trees. "We know you're in there. Come out with your hands up!"

Still no answer was forthcoming from the silent home.

Adele bit her lip, but then gestured toward Leoni and pointed toward the rope ladder. The two of them stepped forward, now moving into the shadow of the elevated home, searching around the ground for something, anything they might use to snare the rope ladder.

Eventually, Leoni nudged her and pointed at a toppled bough. The tree branch was long, but unruly.

Adele retrieved the branch with her partner. Still no sounds were forthcoming from the house. Clearly, Mr. Von Ziegler was hoping they would just leave him alone. But the author's own words propelled her motions. She remembered what he'd written on his website. Rants against tourists. Vicious diatribes seemingly siding with the killer. Which, if their theory held true about Mr. Von Ziegler's nighttime activities, would make sense.

Leoni broke off a couple of the more unruly side branches from the main shaft of wood. Then, together, in one of the strangest breaching efforts Adele had ever been a part of, they moved beneath the house, out from its shadow, and faced the rope ladder. Leoni poked the long branch up, snagging the rope and tugging it.

After couple of tries, the ladder tumbled over the edge and fell, swaying and swinging beneath the elevated home.

Adele held a finger to her lips and tapped Leoni's service weapon, pointing up. Leoni drew his weapon, took a couple of steps back, aimed toward the door and the windows above, providing cover, and then nodded once.

Adele grabbed the rope ladder and began to climb, pulling herself up, feeling the rough texture of the binding beneath her fingers. The sunlight above kept peeking from behind the elevated home in rhythm with the swaying ladder.

Adele pulled herself up the last rung, grunting a bit from the unfamiliar motion of the precarious handhold. She pressed her palm against the firm wood of the floorboards above, and pulled herself onto the platform which elevated the treehouse.

After a moment, she stepped to the side, giving Leoni a clear shot at the door. She pulled her own weapon from her holster, feeling her fingers a bit numb from where they'd gouged into the rough rope. She winced, shaking out a hand, but then, readjusting her grip on her weapon, she pointed it toward the door.

Her eyes flicked to the nearest window. No movement. Darkened by a curtain within and a film of tint on the glass itself.

She pounded her fist against the metal frame of the door and shouted, "Mr. Von Ziegler, open up!"

For the first time, she heard movement. The sound was like a quiet curse, and then the patter of footsteps. But the door didn't open.

"Adrian Von Ziegler," she snapped. "Interpol. Open the door now!"

Leoni still had his weapon trained on the windows, and Adele was preparing to push through the door. But then, a second later, as she reached a hand toward the knob, the door sprang open, nearly knocking her off the platform. Her gun was sent skittering to the floor.

A blur of motion caught her eye, as she reeled back, trying to regain her balance. A figure flung themselves toward the rope ladder and began to scramble down. By the looks of things, they were wearing gloves, and slid down the rope with practiced ease.

Adele cursed and took two skipping steps to grab her gun, and then aimed over the rope ladder.

Mr. Von Ziegler was on the run, and barreled forward, heading toward the trees, ignoring Leoni.

"Stop!" Leoni shouted in English.

But the runner ignored him. Leoni aimed, sighted in—Adele's heart skipped a beat—but then her partner cursed, stowed his weapon, and broke into a sprint, racing after the fleeing man. Adele couldn't descend the ladder as fast as the culprit had. She wasn't wearing gloves, and if she tried to slide, she would rip up her palms. So as she moved down, she could hear the sound of the fleeing man disappearing into the trees.

She cursed. She reached halfway, then dropped, landing with a dull thump on the ground. She took a moment to catch her bearings, glimpsed the form of Leoni's suit as he raced through the trees, and broke into a sprint herself.

She stowed her own weapon and raced across the detritus-scattered floor. Small branches cracked underfoot, the smell of fresh leaves and earth filling the air. She ducked beneath branches, moving deeper into the sparse undergrowth of the more maintained section of forest. The further they went, the harder it would be to move.

She heard shouting now, yelling.

She spotted Leoni, his gun raised, pointing it at a man whose back was pressed to a tree. It looked like he'd caught his sweater in a tangle of thorny shrubs, and was wincing and wailing, trying to extricate himself without doing damage.

"Stop!" Adele shouted. She hurried forward, her own gun rising.

The man snared in the shrubs glanced desperately from Leoni to Adele, his wide eyes bugged out from wrinkled features; his hair was slick without a single strand of white. His hair was that of a young man, but his features were that of someone in their sixties. He had moved far too quickly, though, in Adele's estimation, to be much older than forty. Those were the wrinkles and lines of a man weathered by the weight of the world. Worry lines.

Mr. Von Ziegler was shouting now, trying to shake his tangled arm, but wincing as the thorns ripped through his sweater and skin.

"We're with Interpol," Adele said, firmly. "We need to ask you a few questions."

The Austrian author turned from Leoni to regard her. He was trim, with the proportions of a runner, but his wrinkled, worried face was tinged with red. He tried to speak and slurred his words, suggesting perhaps he'd been drinking. In lightly accented English, he replied, "What do you thugs want from me?"

"To talk," Adele said, firmly. "Lower the branch."

His free hand had snared a sharp stick, which wasn't large enough to be used as a club, nor sharp enough to be used as a skewer, but she didn't want to take any risks.

Mr. Von Ziegler glanced desperately between the two agents as he finally managed to rip his sleeve from the snaring thorn bush, but then, when he glanced over his shoulder toward the deeper parts of the forest, he realized the futility of trying to run through the trees. There was nowhere to go without overgrowth and underbrush.

At last, he sighed, his cheeks still rosy, his eyes bloodshot. He tossed his branch off to the ground and slowly raised his hands.

Leoni and Adele moved in quickly, and, within seconds, they had Mr. Von Ziegler cuffed and began leading him away, back beneath the shadow of his treehouse and toward the waiting vehicle with the Austrian police officer.

"What's this about?" Mr. Von Ziegler said, his words slurred.

"I think you know," said Leoni, pushing the man forward, not roughly, but with a guiding hand toward the waiting cruiser. They managed to maneuver the cuffed man into the back seat of the squad car, and waited for the Austrian police officer to take his driver's seat again. Leoni would sit in the back with the suspect, and Adele in the front. Before she shut the door, though, Adele looked at Mr. Von Ziegler. His bloodshot eyes gazed out at her, equal parts scared and belligerent.

"You're fools, all of you. I didn't do this, whatever you think I did. I'm not a criminal!"

Adele frowned. "Perhaps not. But you have intimate knowledge of three crime scenes where we found bodies. According to your website, it almost seems like you're glad the victims were killed."

His bloodshot eyes blinked a couple of times, and his rosy cheeks twitched. Then his eyes suddenly widened in a slow, snail's pace of realization. His words were still slurred as he said, "The Monument Killer? You're joking. That wasn't me!"

"We'll talk down at the station, watch yourself."

Adele slammed the door shut, cutting off Mr. Von Ziegler before turning and moving around the hood of the car toward the front seat.

He fit the bill. Was he the killer, though? And if he was, would she be able to prove it?

CHAPTER TWENTY ONE

The interrogation room they'd been provided in the Austrian precinct was large enough for Leoni to pace the back of the room, while Adele sat in the chair opposite their travel expert. They had confirmed Mr. Von Ziegler's identity, bringing up a picture from a previous arrest record for a drunk and disorderly.

"Mr. Von Ziegler," Adele said, softly, "I appreciate you coming in with us."

He snorted, but didn't comment.

"We wish to talk to you about some of your more recent website posts. Are you the author of *Days Away: A Travel Guide to Europe*?"

Mr. Von Ziegler crossed his arms and glared out at her from beneath hooded eyes. His wrinkled features were stretched, and his bloodshot gaze had narrowed. "So what if I am? It's not a crime. It's just like the government to try and censor speech! That's what this is. You'll hear from my lawyer!"

"We hope to," Adele said. "But we're not interested in the book. We're interested in the comments you made about the Monument Killer's victims. We're wondering what you have been doing over the last few days."

The eccentric travel expert snorted, leaning back in the metal chair. He tapped his feet against the floor and muttered a few choice insults beneath his breath before saying, "I need a drink. You want me to talk, I need to clear my mind."

Adele glanced at Leoni, who gave a small shake of his head. She looked back at Mr. Von Ziegler and said, "Tell us what we want to know, then you get you a drink."

"Something strong," he said.

"Water," she retorted.

"Then I'm not talking."

"Are you sure you don't want to? Is this you?" She reached to the table, picked up her phone to the prepared screenshot, and began to narrate from the most recent post on Mr. Von Ziegler's website. *"...and while taking the life of anyone might be frowned on by most, only a couple hundred years ago, such treatment of places like this would end in a far more painful death than what these sheep suffered."* She looked up. "Was that you?"

He glared back at her, seemingly caught between his boycott of questions until he was given something to drink and a flicker of recognition at his own web post.

Even half drunk, the author seemed to realize it didn't paint him in a particularly good light.

"You're a heavy drinker, sir," said Leoni, stopping his pacing long enough to lean over Adele and look across the table at their suspect. "You had several public outbursts in the last few months, drunken tirades against tourists if I'm not mistaken."

The man shrugged. "Just because people are disrespectful, stupid, doesn't mean I kill them."

Adele shook her head. "Well, I still would like you to tell me if you were anywhere in the last week or so. As an author, I imagine it's easy for you to go weeks without seeing anyone."

He grunted and stared at his fingers, crossing them in front of each other.

She waited and could feel Leoni pacing again behind her.

"So what?" he said. "I was at home. Getting my work done. That's not a crime. No more tourist books," he said, grunting. "Fiction now. Thrillers." He smiled in a gritted teeth sort of way. "Can't deal with tourists anymore. Selfish, self-absorbed, littering, obnoxious bastards. All of them."

Adele swallowed. She hadn't expected him to be so forthcoming. For someone who prided himself on his ability with words, he sure wasn't careful with them.

"Are you telling me you have no alibi for the last week?"

"I'm telling you," he said, his voice still a bit slurred, "that I am an *author.*"

He said the last word with a flourish of his voice, as if presenting something fascinating, or alluring, like the climax of a magic trick.

Adele was unimpressed. "So you were cooped up in your home, writing, is that what you're saying?"

"I don't chase the muse, the muse chases me," he replied.

Adele was beginning to dislike him for entirely separate reasons than the potential of being a suspected murderer. "Right, so no alibi. A history of tirades against tourists, and direct ties to victims of the last

111

three murders. You wanted to see them dead. You practically gloated."

"I did not gloat," he snapped.

Adele scrolled to the next screenshot on her phone, quoting again, *"A noose is far too good an end for such desecraters as these. Were I the one to snuff their lights, it would be with the full vengeance and fury of Ares..."*

"I don't remember that," he said, surly now.

Adele pushed away from the table. "If you have no alibi, no explanation for those posts, I'm afraid we're going to have to keep you here for little bit longer. Your place will be searched."

"Bah!" he snapped. "You won't find anything there."

Adele hesitated, frowning at this odd phrasing. *You won't find anything there.* Not *I have nothing to hide.* Not *you won't find anything.* Rather, he'd said, *You won't find anything* there.

"Where might we find something then?" Adele said, cautiously.

But Mr. Von Ziegler seemed to realize he'd said too much. He just snorted in her direction and then dipped his head into his hands, his fingers pushing against his dyed locks, tangling in the thin mess.

"Mr. Von Ziegler," Adele said, quietly. "You need to talk with me. Help me clear your name."

No response, just quiet muttering about a drink.

"Mr. Von Ziegler?" she prompted.

But he no longer reacted to her words, still stooped, still muttering at the metal table.

Adele shared a look with Leoni, shrugged, and the two of them stepped away from the table. They waited to see if the motion would elicit an action from Mr. Von Ziegler.

You won't find anything there.

But he kept his head dipped.

"We'll be back soon, Mr. Von Ziegler," Adele said.

Still no response.

Adele sighed and moved out from behind the interrogation desk, across the spacious room and to the door. She tapped on the window, and it unlocked from the outside, allowing the two of them out into the Austrian precinct, as the door clicked shut behind them.

As Leoni and Adele moved toward the sliding doors at the end of the precinct, past the sergeant's desk, Leoni said, in a low tone, "He seems like he might be the guy."

"Seems like it."

"No alibi. All the motive in the world. And definitely has the means."

"Yep. He does seem like it."

"So, how come you don't sound convinced?"

Adele opened her eyes wide, as if testing against a headache from the bright lights in the precinct. She winced a bit, but then glanced toward Agent Leoni and shrugged. "I don't know," she said, softly. "No reason. No good reason at least."

Leoni returned her gaze. "Well, he's the suspect we have. I know my higher-ups at AISE are going to want to speak with him. You might want to call your people. Keep them in the loop."

Adele breathed heavily, but nodded. She didn't love the idea of having to contact Ms. Jayne so soon. But what else could she do? The man had all but admitted to the crime. No alibi, no defense. Not even an attempt to gloss over the violent words he'd spewed on his website. It wasn't a good look. And yet, somehow, she couldn't shake the horrible sensation they were missing something.

Still, she lifted her phone, dialed Ms. Jayne's number, and waited for an answer.

CHAPTER TWENTY TWO

"Yes?" she said, trying not to bite her tongue.

"Agent Sharp?" came Ms. Jayne's voice, louder than usual, with background noise like the sound of a churning fan. "Can you hear me?"

"Yes?" she repeated, deciding not to ask about the noise. Ms. Jayne's business was her own.

"I've been notified you have a suspect in custody. He looks good for it, yes?"

"I... I'm not sure."

"No, Adele, he does. I've been briefed. Good work, Agent."

Adele gnawed on her lip, moving out of the precinct now and taking the steps to the parking lot in search of a bit more privacy. She neared her parked car in the darkening evening, keys jingling as she pulled them from her pocket.

"I—I don't think we have the right angle, Ms. Jayne."

The background noise grew louder and the Interpol correspondent responded, but Adele couldn't make out her words. She winced and said, "What was that?"

Ms. Jayne's voice came crackling and disrupted, but Adele made out the words, "Nonsense. You've done well. Make sure they keep him overnight, understand?"

"Yes, I will. But look—"

The loud noise suddenly cut short, the phone began to beep. Adele blinked, said, "Hello? Hello, Ms. Jayne?"

No response.

"Damn reception," Adele muttered, sliding into the front seat of the car all the same and rolling down the window.

Adele sat in the parking lot outside the Austrian precinct, beneath the glowing yellow of a curved safety light above the asphalt. She reclined in the car, the seat leaned back, her head pressed against the cushioned headrest. Her arm poked out the window into the cool evening air. The summer had gone, slipping away and conceding to night. The darkness in the sky spread out over the city, over the precinct, consuming shadows and settling thick.

Adele stared through the windshield, facing the precinct. A couple of officers also came down the stairs, one of them with a briefcase slung over her shoulder, and another brushing a long strand of hair behind her ear, as she then hefted her heavy belt with tools and weapons and cuffs, and adjusted her uniform, preparing to go on night patrol.

Leoni was still in the precinct, working on paperwork and communicating with the higher-ups in Italy.

As for Adele, she couldn't shake the feeling that they'd missed a step.

Everyone seemed to agree. Ms. Jayne had agreed. Leoni agreed. Leoni's higher-ups had agreed. Authorities from Paris, Italy, and Greece all seemed to agree.

They had their man. They'd captured him.

No questions asked. Simple.

And yet, Adele wasn't convinced.

The killer had been smart. One step ahead. Mr. Von Ziegler, though an author, the sort that might be good enough with words to create riddles, was a drunk. A blowhard. The sort of person to scatter their thoughts across the Internet for everyone to see. He didn't even have an alibi for the murders. And when he tried to run when they'd shown up, there hadn't even been an escape plan. He'd caught himself on thistles.

That didn't have the ring of a criminal mastermind to her.

Absentmindedly, Adele rolled her fingers, tapping them against the vehicle, feeling the cool metal beneath her fingertips. She watched as the two officers on the steps bid farewell and then moved off to their vehicles.

The lights glowing from inside the precinct combated the darkness around, trying to keep it at bay, but failing, casting long shadows and deep alcoves across the parking lot behind the cars.

And yet, Adele appreciated the shadows. The sorts of places one might hide.

The killer had known shadows. The killer had known the Sistine Chapel, had known the Acropolis, had known Notre Dame. The killer had known how to be undetected, how to move quietly. The killer had been smart.

And while innately Adele considered all killers to be stupid at their core, they weren't stupid in the way that would manifest in being caught so easily. Stupid in what they valued. Stupid in how they

115

behaved. Stupid in how they treated others. Yes. But stupid enough to be caught like this? To not even construct an alibi?

She rolled her eyes, closing them, and grunting at the ceiling of the cop car.

"Too easy," she muttered to herself.

Or maybe she just wanted it to be too easy. Maybe she didn't want the case to be over. Because if this case was over, it meant she would have to go back to France. And she wasn't ready to face that particular mess. A copycat killer on the loose, her mother's killer somewhere, hiding, like a puppet-master playing with strings.

She forced her mind away from this train of thought. She wasn't trying to avoid anything. She was simply trying to do her job. But even as she thought it, it wasn't convincing. Still, she summoned to mind the last riddle. Running it over again and again. Two couplets, the language poetic, but also hinting, coy. It seemed to know something, and wanted to tease her with it. The riddle itself was a mockery.

Mr. Von Ziegler was a writer, but bombastic and straightforward. Clever wasn't how she'd describe him, neither was coy.

She ran the riddle through her mind again, and again.
Round eyes in round hands,
my longing for you has grown,
Squares in circles once,
My heart is cast in stone

She thought of Leoni studying the crime scenes, memorizing the information. Where could she possibly start? There were so many options. A list upon list of hundreds of potential places. According to the DGSI's and Interpol's combined resources nearly two hundred locations fit the clue worldwide. A hundred in Europe. A needle in a haystack.

And yet, the clues were there. Hidden, but there.

When it came down to it, though, she had to trust her gut. Which meant what?

She frowned softly, wrinkling her brow, thinking. Then realized.

It meant this *wasn't* about tourism. It wasn't about an industry. This wasn't about the location. It was about something else.

Which meant what?

Which meant that to think like the killer, she had to think like a fanatic. To think like someone obsessed. Not like an avenging angel,

116

not like a disgruntled worker, or a violent protester. This wasn't a conservationist. And, if she was right, it wasn't some angry author who wrote a tour book.

This was something else. Something else entirely. She considered it a moment longer, and then realized the key.

All the locations had religious roots. Which meant, on the lists she'd been given of potential locations, anything that was a tourist attraction without religious overtones could be forgotten, discarded. No museums, no remnants of wars, no architectural spectacles.

She went to her phone, pulled out the list, and began scanning. Things like the Eiffel Tower or Statue of Liberty, these could be easily ignored.

But then again, she didn't know enough about these places herself. She cycled to her phone, lifted it, calling Leoni.

For a moment, no response, and then, after a couple of rings, her partner's voice said, "Agent Sharp?"

"I need you in the parking lot."

"Now?"

"Yeah. Paperwork can wait. I have an idea. Have a second?"

"Yes. I'm coming."

Simple. Polite. *Yes, I'm coming.* A strange bird Agent Leoni.

She waited, tapping her fingers against the metal of the car, watching as Leoni emerged from the precinct doors. A few seconds later, he took the stairs, looked around, spotted her, then began to move toward her.

As he approached the side of the door, she gestured around toward the driver's seat. He didn't hesitate or protest, merely rounded the car, sliding into the front seat next to her. He looked at her, waiting, polite and quizzical.

"Know that list we got, from the new riddle? The one from Interpol?"

"Yes."

"You've been studying it, yeah? You know a lot about that stuff."

"I try."

"I need you to tell me which ones are the most religious. Not a specific religion. And keep it to Europe, but which ones are the most religious? Preferably very old."

He frowned at her. "I'm not sure exactly how to quantify—"

"Ignore the tourist angle. Ignore anything that doesn't have

117

religious overtones. Which ones are holy sites? Even if the tenants of the religion are long dead."

Leoni shrugged, but then began flipping through his phone, his eyebrows lowered. He frowned, muttering to himself as he did, and saying things like, "Maybe. No. Not that one. No. Definitely this one. Could be this one. How about this one. No. No."

He continued to cycle through, and after a few minutes he stopped and looked at her.

"How many?"

"Twenty," he replied.

She winced. "Twenty?"

"Well, ten for sure and ten maybes."

"All right, for the sake of argument, let's forget the maybes. So there's ten that could be overtly religious that apply to the riddle."

He nodded. "At least according to the experts."

She studied his face. "What do you mean by that?"

"I mean, the word he uses here, *hearts* cast *in stone,* they took to just mean stone. But he's specific here, when you look, that it is *not* stone hewn by tools. It's a *heart* cast in stone. Something organic, yes? A heart is like a tree is like a bird. An organ. Natural. Not chiseled or stained or painted… I don't think he's talking about just any old stone."

Adele could feel her pulse quickening. "What do you think he means?"

"I think he means weathered stone. Stone that is exposed to the elements. But not an external feature, rather a core element. Remember in the other riddles, the one about the virgin? The core part of it was included in the middle couplet."

"So what does that mean?"

He scrolled down her phone and then tapped on a single word on the list. "The others are made of stone, glass, metal, support beams. Not this, though. I think it's this one. This is where Mr. Von Ziegler was going to strike."

She leaned in, looking over the top of his finger.

Stonehenge.

She stared at the word and felt a flutter in her stomach. "That's a religious site?" she asked.

Leoni looked at her, seemingly surprised, but quickly covered and said, "Yes, actually. It was a sacrificial spot for druids, centuries ago."

"You're sure?" she said, her back prickling.

118

"No, not sure. No one is. But that's one of the running theories. A popular theory."

"And on your list narrowed down; the ten that could apply—this one's the one with exposed stone... Round eyes in round hands... Squares made circle..." Adele raised her eyebrows. "Stonehenge is in a circle, yes? The monoliths are rounded but also placed in a round circle."

"Exactly."

Adele nodded, her head bobbing. "That's it then."

"Maybe. But Mr. Von Ziegler isn't saying. I could spring it on him. Maybe try to get his reaction."

Adele shook her head though. "This isn't about Mr. Von Ziegler. I don't think we have the killer."

Leoni blinked.

She pressed on, taking his silence as permission. "I think we caught the wrong guy. It's just too easy. He's not as clever as this murderer. He's a bombastic drunk."

"If this isn't the guy, who is?"

Adele tapped the line reading *Stonehenge*. "I think we'll find him there. Maybe even tonight. I think he's going to kill again, soon."

Leoni stared at her, and this time she didn't speak, allowing her words to do their work. Silence hung between them for a moment, and then Leoni heaved a soft breath. "That's impossible; everyone thinks we have him. I just spoke to your correspondent from Interpol—"

"Ms. Jayne?"

Leoni bobbed his head. "She congratulated me on a job well done."

Adele wrinkled her brow. "I didn't know she was going to call you."

"AISE thinks we've succeeded here too. They're going to be flying us home tomorrow morning."

But Adele was shaking her head vehemently now, her hands back in the car, clasped in her lap. "We can't do that," she said, hurriedly. "We don't have the killer. Please, Leoni, I know you don't know me well. I need you to trust me, though. This is the right guy, whoever the killer is, they're still out there. And they're going to be at Stonehenge."

Leoni winced. "A guess," he said. "*My* guess. And I'm not confident. Why are you?"

"I'm confident this is supposed to be a religious spot. I'm confident that you know enough that this is our best shot. A sacrificial spot for

119

druids," she said. "Organic stone… Like a heart. It makes some sense. I know it isn't perfect… I get it. But it's the best shot we have. Our job is best done in matters of degree."

"Maybe if you reverse engineer the riddle, but only—"

"The riddle. Exactly. And that's what we've done every time. Looking back, it's been obvious. Well, imagine we're standing in Stonehenge right now, we reread the riddle. Looking back, it would be obvious, wouldn't it?"

Leoni reached up, scratching his head. "I mean, maybe. I don't know. I guess probably."

"I can work with *probably*. All right, well, give me a second. Can you trust me on this?"

Leoni hesitated, but to his credit, the hesitation didn't last long. At last, he just dipped his head and said, "I can do that."

Adele raised her phone again and quickly cycled to Ms. Jayne's number. She called for the second time that day, and waited, the phone ringing.

It was night, and she hoped the Interpol correspondent would answer. Thankfully, after another few rings, the phone vibrated, shaking her hand, and Ms. Jayne's voice came out on the speaker. "Agent Sharp?"

Adele cleared her throat. "Ms. Jayne? Hello, do you have a moment?"

"Yes. Is this about the case?"

"About the one in Austria."

"The suspect didn't get away, did he?" she said, hurriedly.

"No," Adele said, quickly. She looked up at Leoni and shared a nervous look. "Nothing like that. But look, Ms. Jayne, I just wanted to say, I don't think we have the right guy. I've been talking to Agent Leoni, and we think that if we narrow down the list, the most likely next spot—"

"Agent Sharp, let me stop you there. I spoke with Christopher earlier. Smart man. Both of you did a good job here. How about you take the accolades and don't ruin it."

Adele winced. Clearly, Ms. Jayne didn't want to hear any more. But she had to. "I know how important it is to solve this one. I know there's a lot of money behind the tourist industries. I know there's a lot of people who are glad that we caught the guy. But I don't think we did. We don't have enough evidence to know for sure. And a lack of alibis isn't the same as being guilty."

"Do you have other evidence of another suspect?"

"No, not like that, but—"

"You have no new evidence. So why exactly are you calling me?"

"Look, we need a flight to Stonehenge. Can we have that arranged?"

There was a soft sigh on the other end of the phone that sounded like someone exhaling through their nose. Ms. Jayne had always been reasonable, clever, and she knew how to employ Adele's skills where needed. But she was also in charge of a lot of other agents. Juggling plates. And this time, she said, "I'm afraid not, Agent Sharp. We already have you booked on a plane ride back to Paris. Executive Foucault wishes to speak with you. Besides, how would it look if I sent off an Italian agent with you, signaling to his government and everyone else that we don't have any confidence in the suspect we're detaining? That'll get out. Lawyers will hear about it. It'll be the first thing the defense uses. That we didn't even believe we had the right suspect. Now isn't the time for a show of weakness. I'm sorry. I expect you on the first flight back to Paris."

"But—"

"I'm sorry, Adele. That's final. Is there anything else?"

Adele stammered, then sighed. "I guess not. But I think you're wrong."

"I appreciate all input. If you have anything more to say to me, please call back tomorrow morning. Have a good night. And good job."

Ms. Jayne hung up.

Adele sighed, sitting in the car, her fingers tapping again against the cool metal of the exterior through the window. Leoni was looking at her sympathetically. "I guess they think it's closed."

She stared back, glaring now. Her blood pulsed and her cheeks prickled with frustration. "It isn't. Someone is going to die tonight. Tomorrow morning will be too late." She paused, thinking desperately, then said, "How long will it take to drive there?"

"Stonehenge? Too long." Leoni glanced out the window, but then looked back. He seemed to be weighing Adele, gauging her with an appraising look. At last, he sighed, softly, and said, "We don't have to drive."

He spoke quietly, his voice nearly a whisper, but it was like a lifeline, thrown to a drowning victim, catching her attention all the same against a sea of chaos. "Excuse me?"

Leoni breathed once, then spoke louder. "I have a friend; he lives about an hour from here. An old associate of mine. Remember how I told you my mother used to be an agent?"

"I remember."

"Well, her third ex-husband runs charter flights out of Austria."

Adele stared, dumbfounded. "You are actually James Bond," she said.

He looked at her confused, but then pressed on. "He always used to like me. I think if we ask, he'll give us a flight. But that's the best I can do. Just this once. If we don't find anyone there, I'm going to have to consider the case closed as well."

Adele nodded feeling her chest skip a beat. "We'll find the killer. Trust me." Even as she said it, she thought, *Do I even trust myself?* She shook off the niggling doubt. "We need that flight right away."

CHAPTER TWENTY THREE

Agent John Renee glanced at the crossed-off names on his list, the small note paper illuminated by the light growing from the center of the sidewalk. The door to the Cadillac was ajar, and one of John's long legs dangled past into the street. His eyes narrowed vaguely as he studied the list of ten names. Six of them crossed off. Only four left.

He sighed. No red flags, solid alibis for the first six. Was he running out of road?

For a moment, John missed Adele. She was the sort to run down grueling leads, one at a time. Once, she'd walked an entire street, looking for a security camera, then spent hours combing through the footage. Nothing tired that woman out.

John, though, missed his distillery. He missed the quiet, careful life of a man who only cared the minimum amount. But that wasn't an option this time.

He shifted, rising from inside the vehicle and stepping onto the curb. The Parisian air was warm and still. John rubbed at his jaw. No minimum effort this time, not where Adele was concerned. Her mother had been killed by this bastard. Copycat, or otherwise, whoever had sent those notes to Elise Romei had eventually ripped her to ribbons.

Nearly a decade ago, Adele had failed to track the killer. And now, she was off in Italy, then Greece. Unwilling to return, to face the case. And John didn't blame her. But it meant it was up to him to solve this for her. If he let her down, there'd be no chance of reconnecting, no chance of... anything.

Besides, she deserved this. If anyone deserved a win, it was Adele.

John glanced at his marked piece of notepad paper, studying the next name on the list. Andrew Maldonado. The guy was too jumpy, too nervous not to know something. No—he'd been holding out. If anyone on the list was suspect, it was Mr. Maldonado.

John folded the piece of paper across the four indented square sections, and then tucked the list into his pocket. He pulled out his phone, checking the email he'd requested. Records for Mr. Maldonado. And an address.

He confirmed the location, then glanced up at the small, two-story home in the center of Vitry-sur-Seine. The lights were off, and the curtains drawn. John stepped along the curb, to the small pathway leading up to the blue metal door. He noted a piece of tape over the doorbell.

John didn't approach the door, though. He wasn't here to announce his presence. No. Playing by the rules? That was Adele's way. John had other tactics. And they'd served him well, long before he'd met Agent Sharp.

He circled around the house now, half-crouched, shooting glances toward the streets. His head dipped below the windows as he lowered his large frame and then, every few moments, looked up, peeking through the first window.

But the glass set in the aluminum siding was dark; still no lights and again shuttered by a curtain. He heard a quiet screech and stiffened, glancing sharply over his shoulder. A car trundled past, and he could hear music blaring from the open windows. The vehicle didn't stop, though, and the headlights flashed, disappearing around the T-intersection at the end of the street.

John breathed a shallow puff, then moved on to the next window. His feet padded against damp grass next to a large, whirring air-conditioning unit. He paused by the next window and peered into the house. For a moment, he thought he heard something. Movement? A quiet whimper?

His spine tingled and John's hand instinctively went to his gun. But again, though he pressed his cheek against the cool glass, he couldn't see inside the house.

Picking up the pace a bit, still half-crouched, he made his way around the back of the house, coming face to face with a sliding glass door next to a series of plants in ceramic pots. Then John froze.

A light was on inside, pulsing in the kitchen. No curtain on the glass door. The fence behind the yard was large enough to block any prying eyes.

And the scene that confronted him was like something out of a nightmare.

A figure was standing over another person. The first figure held something glinting in their right hand and wore black gloves and a black face mask, now lowered to their chin. Andrew?

The second person lay on the kitchen table. Their hands were bound to the tops of the chairs which were wedged beneath the table. Their shirt was missing and their chest was covered in blood.

"Merde!" John cursed and his instincts kicked in a micro-second later. He'd been right about Mr. Maldonado! The factory worker was in the middle of killing someone *right now!*

John shouted, raised his gun, fired twice. But Andrew was quick. He spun as the glass window shattered and crystalline shards scattered over the ground. He gripped his knife, speckling blood drops across the kitchen floor. For a moment, a pale face peered out over the lowered mask. John stared into the eyes of the killer.

"Stop!" John screamed.

But Andrew ignored him, turning on his heel and bolting to safety, behind the table laden with his victim. John shouted, but Andrew darted through the only available door remaining—into the pantry. The door clicked shut a second later and John rushed into the house, squeezing off another shot, but the bullet slammed into the wall next to the now sealed pantry door.

John felt his heart hammering in his chest. He could hear the sound of scrambling in the small closet space. For a moment, he thought to bully his way through the door, flinging his body at the wooden barricade. But what if Maldonado was armed?

John breathed a shallow sigh, listening to the sounds of movement turning to quiet stillness. Still staring at the sealed door, he heard a faint dripping and looked back to the kitchen table, watching as a line of crimson streaked down the surface of the table, spilled over the edge, and fell, tumbling one droplet at a time to splash across the tiled floor.

John gritted his teeth. The figure on the table moved again, groaning in pain. He was on a timer.

"You're trapped in there," John howled toward the pantry door. "Come out with your hands up!"

No sounds were forthcoming. For a moment, John wondered if perhaps there was an exit he hadn't seen in the brief moments he'd glimpsed the interior of the food storage space. Amidst the cereal boxes, the noodles, and the dry goods, was there a back exit? He'd never heard of such a thing. No, he decided. The killer was still in there playing possum.

"I'm serious," John said, growling. "I know you're in there. Come out with your hands up, now, or I'm going to start shooting at the door and plug you through the wood."

He raised his gun, aiming, deciding to go center mass, and then take another couple of shots toward the base of the door in case the killer had gone prone on the ground.

He heard another couple of dripping sounds, and wanted to scream. He had to hurry. The victim was bleeding out. But on the other hand, if he let the killer get away, Adele would never forgive him. He knew, deep in his bones, deep near where certainty was born, that he had found her mother's killer. There was no other explanation.

Suddenly, a soft, lilting voice probed out from the dark pantry, through the shut wooden door, and John shivered at the sound. There was just something too calm, too cajoling about that voice. It was the voice of a kindly teacher, a mother at play with her children. The voice of a favorite older brother or sister. The gender was hard to determine. It was a high-pitched, lilting voice.

"Agent Renee," came the voice, followed by a soft sigh. "Is that you?"

The chills along John's spine only increased at the creepy tone of voice. The prickles had now reached his cheeks, and he resisted the urge to scream.

"Maldonado, come out of there now!"

"We could be friends, you know. We have a friend in common, you and I."

"Shut up," John howled. He wasn't in the mood for games. "Come out here with your hands up."

"She's very marked, you know," the voice continued as if it hadn't heard John. "Do you think she knows you're here? Do you think she can sense it? I've often wondered at that sort of thing."

John kept his gun on the door and stepped forward. For one sickly moment, though, he decided that if he flung open the door, and the man inside was armed, then he would be putting himself in danger.

He heard the low, croaking groan of the victim behind him on the table. He heard the tap of crimson droplets against the tiled floor, as if increasing in tempo, suggesting his time was nearly fully spent.

"He is still alive," said the soft voice. "You should call for help. He's in a bad way. He's been through a lot of pain."

"Pain you put him through, bastard. Get out here now!" John was tired of asking and squeezed off a shot through the wooden door; splinters flew everywhere, a bullet hole punching through the center of the frame.

The voice continued as if it hadn't even heard the gunshot.

"You think you could deliver a message to her—I mean, of course, after I get away and you're left here, desperate and frustrated with yourself."

"You're cocky, aren't you? Let's see if you can get away from this."

John fired two more shots. This time toward the floor, in case the killer had gone prone, but again, the killer's voice kept coming from the pantry. The door, now punctured with holes, with splinters strewn across the ground, creaked open on old hinges. The door stood ajar, just enough to give John a glimpse of the shadows within. But not so much he could make out movement from inside the small compartment.

"You really should be careful. Our friend on that table doesn't have much time left. We were playing together for nearly an hour before you showed up."

John shivered at the sound. He felt a prickle meet the shiver along his spine. Fear in different forms, and yet, a fear he recognized. The scar across his chin itched, and the fear increased. But John had been in these situations before. He wasn't about to let some deranged man get into his mind.

"I'm warning you, come out, *now*."

"Do you remember Gerard?" said the voice.

John went stiff. His shoulder blades pressed against the counter, and he could feel his own chest thumping, his chin jutting forward now, his eyes wide, unblinking.

"What did you say?"

"Gerard; he was your copilot, wasn't he? Six of you in total, wasn't it? Does it weigh on you? You call me a monster, Agent Renee. But you've killed more people than I have. And you enjoy it, too, don't you? I can always tell. You dirty dog." The voice was laughing now.

John roared, and surged to his feet now. He wasn't sure how Maldonado knew the names of his deceased brother copilot. That information about the helicopter crash was classified.

With a bellow like a wounded grizzly, John surged toward the shut door, flung open the frame, and pointed his gun into the dark.

Nobody on the floor. None sidled against the shelves. He stared, breathing heavily for a moment.

He heard a soft, quiet giggle still emanating from within the room, but the closed, shadowed nature of the pantry made it difficult for him to place the source of the sound. The laughter grew louder, and John

127

cursed, gun raised as he stepped into the pantry, his weapon pointing toward a particularly dark portion behind the stack of old cereal boxes.

And then John heard movement before he saw it. His eyes flicked up. Impossible. Too small. The person couldn't have been much larger than a child to fit into the space on the top shelf to his left. Just over the door, out of sight. Two eyes stared back—one of them strange, reflecting light in an odd way as if dulled somehow. John didn't have time to take much notice though. In his anger and fury, he'd missed it. The figure dropped fast, moving quick like a snake. John whirled around, squeezing off another shot, but the figure was already darting toward the pantry door, flinging himself through the gap.

With a bellow, John gave chase.

But the figure moved around the side of the pantry, into the distant hall.

John began to run after him, but then heard a particularly loud groan coming from the figure strapped to the kitchen table, still bleeding out, his features slicked with blood, pale. He froze, a prickle of horror spreading down him. He glanced to the table and realized his mistake.

Andrew Maldonado wasn't the killer.

Andrew was bleeding out on the table. He recognized the bearded, pasty-faced man from his visit to the factory. Except his features were even more pale now, and blood stained the underside of his beard. In a weak, whimpering voice, Andrew tried to speak, but couldn't seem to manage it. He started gurgling, his eyes fluttering up. His body was covered in cuts and wounds. Blood stained the table, the floor and even, somehow, the ceiling.

Andrew tried to speak again, straining as he did, the ropes around his wrists and ankles, anchoring him to the chairs wedged beneath the table. He only managed to eke out a single syllable. "…Help."

John heard the flurry of footsteps as the unknown killer beat a retreat toward the door, fleeing the scene. For a moment, John was caught in an impossible choice.

Andrew was still alive, not dead yet. If John pursued the killer, then the factory worker would bleed out. John knew enough field medicine to know he needed direct pressure on Maldonado's bigger cuts, immediately, followed by a series of desperate prayers the ambulance reached them in time. John snarled, hearing the front door slam open, hearing the sound of scampering feet.

He cursed desperately, and then made up his mind, grabbing dishcloths from the counter next to an old microwave and quickly clamping down on the visibly worst injuries.

"Hang on," John muttered. "You're going to be okay. Hang tight."

Andrew gasped again at the pain of the bandages. John used a utility knife to cut the bonds around Andrew's wrists. "Hold this in place if you want to live. This one too. As hard as you can. I know it hurts. Look at me, no *look*. I know it hurts. You're going to die if you don't. Hold them. Now!"

The booming commands of John's voice seemed to jar some consciousness, if only a little, back into Andrew. The factory worker gasped, but with weak fingers did his best to press the cloths to the indicated positions. John kept one hand holding the makeshift bandage against the worst wound and with his other, he fished a phone from his pocket, quickly dialing 112.

"...Help. Please..."

Two words, better than one.

"Trying," John retorted. Then the operator answered. "Hey," John snapped. "Vitry-sur-Seine, house number thirty two, east. Man bleeding out. Agent John Renee, DGSI. Send EMTS *now!*" He then hung up in order to put more pressure on the factory worker's wounds. John clenched his teeth and glanced again toward the now empty hall. He could practically feel the warm night air moving through the house. The killer was gone. Escaped. And John had let it happen. He'd have a hell of a time explaining that one to Adele.

"Who was that?" John demanded. "Hey, listen, tell me. Who the hell was that?"

Andrew's eyes fluttered and he tried to stammer out a response, but couldn't seem to manage.

For a moment, John felt a flash of sympathy. But while he wasn't the bloodhound Adele was, he wasn't stupid either. He could smell a pile of shit eventually. Andrew Maldonado was the seventh name on his list. Out of all the names he'd been given, how come Andrew had been targeted? By a copycat? By the murderer from ten years ago, the one they called the Spade Killer?

He'd been targeted specifically before John could interview him properly. Why?

Because she kicked over the hornet's nest, his subconscious told him. *Because Adele was onto something.*

"Hey!" John snapped. "Tell me who that was, or I'm leaving you here to bleed out." Of course, he knew he wouldn't. But Andrew didn't. John's sympathy only went so far. He'd been through worse injuries than this. He'd been through worse pain. Agony wasn't an excuse. "Tell me who that was!" John demanded.

Andrew stumbled over his words again. But this time, John caught a flicker in the man's eye. Suggesting perhaps there was a spark beneath the facade. Perhaps he wasn't as poorly off as he seemed.

"Don't test me. I'll let you bleed out. I've killed suspects before!" Of course, they'd been shooting at him at the time, but Andrew didn't need to know that.

"No, please," he said, weakly now. A bit more strength in his voice. Not much, but enough.

"Ah, so you can talk. Who was that? How are you involved?"

"I don't know," Andrew gasped.

"Not good enough!" John snapped, twisting one hand on a bandage threateningly.

Andrew whimpered. "Please…"

"No please. *Tell me.*"

A desperate gasp of air, then, his eyes flickering shut, Andrew said, "…Jokes…didn't know… Just jokes…"

Then he passed out.

CHAPTER TWENTY FOUR

Like a butterfly returning to a cocoon, Adele sat entrapped by glass and metal beneath a steady flow of cool air from the nozzles set in the ceiling above. A much smaller plane. But one that Leoni's connection had agreed to loan them, pilot included.

Leoni sat in the cockpit, chatting away with an old friend. Which left Adele in the back, sitting in the first passenger's seat, studying the sky through the window. They were headed to England. Stonehenge.

Defying Ms. Jayne, the Italians, the Greeks, DGSI—everyone. Defiance wasn't natural to Adele, but she could play the part when it was most needed.

She felt a flicker of worry in her gut. She missed John. Missed her old partner.

But now wasn't the time for hang-ups. Now she couldn't afford a mistake. Night was coming quick and she'd gambled someone's life. If she was wrong, and the killer struck somewhere else, then the death was hers to own.

She was the only one who seemed convinced they'd caught the wrong man. But she wasn't as convinced with Stonehenge. It fit the riddle. It did. But... something Leoni had said bothered her.

She gnawed on her lip, sitting perked up, not leaning against the chair, nor leaning too far forward. Her legs weren't crossed, but rather braced, set against the ground as if preparing for impact. She didn't even realize her posture until her back began to cramp.

Adele huffed and leaned back now, glancing through the darkened window. Only a few hours left until midnight. Then, the killer would strike in the dead of night. At Stonehenge? Or somewhere else?

Why was she second-guessing? A lot was on the line. But also... something else.

What was it Leoni had said?

Stonehenge fit the bill, didn't it? It fit her theory about religion and sacrifice, believed to have been a sacrificial spot for druids. But... Leoni had said it was a theory. Unconfirmed. People didn't actually know Stonehenge's use.

Why did that matter?

Because it mattered to the killer. It had to. This wasn't a man playing fiction, nor was it a man playing in half-truths. A theory? Would a theory motivate someone like this? Everyone else operated under the assumption he was targeting tourists. But Adele wasn't nearly so convinced.

She could hear voices talking from the front of the small plane, the cockpit door ajar so she could just see the back half of Leoni's suited form. Even from this angle, he looked handsome. Stonehenge had been his guess. He was smart, brilliant, even. He knew more languages than her, had more connections, probably even a photographic memory.

So why did the guess bother her?

The killer wouldn't desecrate his mission with a *theory*. That's why. Leoni knew facts and information and language. He knew how to relate kindly and politely to decent folk.

But Adele knew the less-than-decent sorts. She knew people. Not normal people. Not good humans. She knew the twisted, nasty, broken sort. She'd been touched by such killers. She'd seen them face to face, again and again. She knew how they thought, a gift given to her nearly a decade ago.

She knew what they wanted.

And it wouldn't be found in a theory.

Which meant what?

It meant the second thought she'd been considering bobbed to the surface of her mind. She had never visited Stonehenge as a child. A popular location, for sure. Her parents, desperate to keep her cultured, despite the family break, had taken her all over Europe. But never to Stonehenge.

However, her father had taken her, once upon a time, to place in Germany. Not nearly as well known. Not the sort that might arouse attention from a global set of gawkers. Not the sort that a tourist industry might fear disruption in.

There was another henge. She could remember it now. She'd been thirteen at the time. Back for a summer to visit her father, briefly. The Pömmelte Henge in Germany. A rather obscure place, sometimes called the "Stonehenge of Germany."

Why did this matter? Why did she think this carried any weight?

"Because," she said, speaking out loud to herself as if in an effort to convince her own mind. "That place isn't a theory. They found more than fifty skeletons buried there."

She nodded to herself, her eyes unblinking, once again sitting upright as she stared at the back of the open cockpit door.

Stonehenge was speculation. The religious implications were *guessed.* Not certain. Pömmelte, on the other hand, was certainly a sacrificial spot.

But it was obscure. No one really knew about this German Stonehenge. So were the bosses right? Was this a tourist angle? If so, the killer's path was clear. The Stonehenge in England would be the obvious target. Everyone knew about it. Postcards, video games, online posts.

But if she was right... if this wasn't about tourism, but about beliefs. About desecration. About something personal to the killer himself...

Then he wouldn't care how many people *knew* the place. In fact, the riddles themselves suggested the killer *liked* being a step ahead. Liked subverting expectations. Liked unpredictability.

Which meant, if Adele was right, he wouldn't be in England tonight. He would be in Pömmelte. No theories, actual skeletons. No legends, an actual history of buried corpses.

She shivered at the thought and reached up, shutting the nozzle to the air flow. Still, she continued to shiver, and wrapped her arms around her, leaning back in the seat. Adele sighed slowly. But maybe it was all in her head.

She'd fled Paris to Germany to avoid a case. Maybe her subconscious was betraying her, trying to avoid a conclusion to this case all the same. Maybe she didn't want to catch the killer... If she could continue the chase, it would allow her to avoid what awaited her back home.

She gnawed on her lip. Ms. Jayne had told her not to be arrogant. And maybe the Interpol boss was right. Adele didn't know everything. She couldn't.

For a moment, she considered stepping to the cockpit, catching the attention of Leoni and his pilot friend, demanding they turn to Germany.

But then she puffed a breath, closed her eyes, and leaned back. Maybe it was all in her head. Ms. Jayne had been doing this sort of thing longer than Adele ever had. Everyone else seemed to think this was about tourism. About spectacle. They were calling him the

Monument Killer, after all.

She breathed and then relaxed, settling in for the rest of the flight. Her mind was just playing tricks. He would be at Stonehenge. He would be in England. Everyone else was probably right.

And though she tried to soothe herself with such thoughts, Adele couldn't help but shake the terrible sensation that they were making a mistake.

But still, she kept her mouth shut. She was too close to it. Too distracted. Maybe it was time to let someone else take the lead. At least in theory.

CHAPTER TWENTY FIVE

Adele stayed to the trees, peering out at the open hilltop in the shadows of the cresting night. At her side, she felt Leoni shift, readjusting and grunting, massaging roughly at one of his legs, which, judging by her own aches, likely had fallen asleep.

She glanced at her watch. 10:32. The pillars of old stone topped by boulders circled the old clearing. Tourists had long since cleared out. The police had been notified of Adele's and Leoni's presence and had even provided a lift from the private airport where they'd landed.

But now, they'd been waiting for near an hour.

Nothing. No sign of the killer. No sign of anything.

Adele leaned back, pressing her back against the bark of the tree where she leaned, staring into the night, eyes peeled, desperately seeking. She could feel Leoni next to her, vigilant, but in a polite way. He wasn't *engaged* in his vigilance, suggesting, perhaps, that he was simply here on her call.

A call, it seemed, that was turning up nothing.

"Anything?" Leoni whispered behind her.

Adele crouched now, wincing and readjusting. A pang in her back from the flight over had intensified and she shifted, trying to find a more comfortable position.

"Not yet," she said.

"Yet?"

"Yet."

"All right," he said, his tone betraying nothing.

She glanced around the old stones, her eyes darting through shadows. No movement. No sound. She'd been wrong. Then again, maybe they were just early. She shifted again, gnawing on her lip. Yes, that had to be it. They were early.

"Do you think—" Leoni began, but Adele snapped, cutting him off.

"I don't know."

Leoni didn't reply this time. Even nice guys have an end to their patience. He breathed a soft sigh and continued to watch, dutiful but detached. Vigilant but with an air of long-suffering.

She missed John. Renee didn't doubt her. They'd been through too much.

But the only reason it mattered, doubt or otherwise, was because she was now doubting herself. She got to her feet now, stretching, pausing for a moment. Then, with a growl of frustration, she stomped forward, heading directly toward the historical site.

"Hang on," Leoni called after her.

She didn't bother to reply. She had to know. She marched up the trail, away from the very sparse tree line, across open flatland and toward the old, towering stones. She felt the wind pick up, moving over the unencumbered terrain, across the flat marshy ground, her feet pressing into the soft grass and the rippled earth, like waves in a pond. Her breath came haggard by the time she reached the landmark. The shadows of the stones swallowed her as she approached, the giant boulders rising, weathered, like pudgy fingers groping at the sky. A slow flicker of awe settled in her gut, but she pushed it aside. Emotions now would only distract.

She stepped into the ring of stones, looking around, desperately seeking.

Nothing. No one. No one approaching, no one in hiding.

She'd been wrong.

Maybe we're just early.

But she shook her head. It felt wrong. It all felt wrong. So why wasn't she trusting her instincts? Did she really think the killer was caught back in Austria? Did she think this was over?

"No," she muttered, firm but with finality.

Standing in the cold, beneath a glaring moon, witnessed only by the night, the circle of massive stones and her Italian partner, Adele stood still. Still was a risk. Still allowed thoughts to rise. And as she stood, surveying the stones, left to her thoughts for the briefest moment of solitude, the familiar creeping chill began to rise up her spine.

She nibbled the corner of her lip and felt an urge to scream, but stoppered the cry. She huffed a breath as images of her mother now flashed across her mind. The images she'd been fleeing. The thoughts she'd hoped to abandon back in Paris. That was stupid. There was no leaving these thoughts behind, not in Paris, not in Germany, not in England in the dead of night.

They were hers. Part of her, latched into her skin as deep as any parasite.

136

She didn't want them to go away. Because they were a reminder, too. A reminder of what was at stake. If she failed, if she guessed wrong, others would be cursed with a decade of torment. Others would have mothers ripped apart and ripped away. No more running.

She didn't shut off the images this time. Instead, she stood straight-backed, tall and firm, watching the scenes flash across her mind's eye. She didn't recoil, nor did she flee. She felt the horror rise in her gut, but weathered the storm.

She stood there, breathing shallowly. Leoni was now calling out to her, but she ignored him. Her feet didn't move, set at shoulder width, a fighter's stance. *Bleeding, bleeding always bleeding.* She saw the wounds, the cuts, the injuries. She saw her mother's lifeless form. She remembered her own scream at the news. Remembered her father sobbing on the phone. Remembered the look of pity and sympathy of the policeman. Remembered the terror, the trembling, horrible, frigid terror that had settled on her shoulders a decade ago and refused to leave.

The fear had made her strong. So why was she doubting herself now?

Another few minutes passed and Leoni was now behind her, trying to catch her attention. He murmured, "Are you all right?"

But she kept her eyes ahead, focused. She could feel the fear fading now. Not suppressed, not thrown aside, not ignored. But fading, receding like a tide. Inevitable in its arrival, but, also, inevitable in its retreat.

A part of her. A part that couldn't be severed. So why had she tried?

And why, now, had she second-guessed herself? Her instincts were honed in a crucible of agony.

"It's not here," she said, softly.

Leoni seemed relieved she was speaking again. "Excuse me?"

"It's not here," she murmured. She glanced back at him, her gaze peering out in the night. The stones around them wreathed the land in shadow, distant lights from traffic and structures glowed in the dark.

"The killer?"

"The crime scene," she said. "The killer isn't here either. I was wrong."

He swallowed. "Well, no shame in trying. I don't blame you. At least we know now that Mr. Von Ziegler—"

But she shook her head, a short jerking motion. Her instincts hadn't failed her before. And she couldn't doubt them now. Perhaps she was wrong. Perhaps everyone else had been right. But Adele wasn't everyone else. She needed to stop being so scared. Scared of Paris. Scared of the higher-ups. Scared of failing.

"It isn't him," she said. "I know it isn't."

Leoni's face was scattered in gloom as he frowned at her, his lovely features bunching. "I thought you just said—"

"This isn't the scene," Adele replied. "I thought so on the plane, but I second-guessed myself. I shouldn't have. The killer is going to Germany."

Leoni gaped at her now. She didn't look at his face, though. It didn't matter. Perhaps he doubted her, perhaps he was exasperated with her, perhaps he was frustrated. But it didn't matter. She could weather his emotions. What mattered was doing what she knew was right. Even if she failed, she had to trust her instincts. She knew killers. She *knew* men like the Monument Killer. She *knew* how they thought. She'd lived, sharing mind space with such folks, for the last ten years.

Some like Leoni were blessed with fiendishly good looks. Some like Ms. Jayne were gifted with the ability to lead, manage, administrate. Some like John were tough as nails, displaying excellence in their chosen craft, be it found in books or with bullets.

Adele, though, had a different gift. Born of pain. It wasn't a gift found in books, nor one earned through experience. It wasn't the sort of gift honed or taught by a doting teacher. No, the tutors of her gift were harsh. And yet it was a gift.

She could think like monsters.

"He doesn't care about this place. Tourism isn't the point."

Leoni sighed. "I know you've said that. But maybe you're wrong."

"I'm not. I don't think so. And if I am, it's my badge anyway. You've been more than helpful. But... I have one last request."

She finally turned, looking Leoni in the eyes.

"What?" he said.

"That pilot friend of yours. I need him to take me to Germany. Right now."

"What... like tonight?"

"Like now."

Leoni stared at her. "I... He has to at least register a flight plan. It could cost him his job if—"

"No time." She shook her head. "No time at all."

"It will cost you *your* job," he said. "If you're wrong, both of you will lose everything."

Another flicker of fear. Another swirl of terror rising like a creeping wave. But she didn't push it away this time. She let it wash over her, allowed it to recede, her skin tingling. "I don't care. Someone's life is at stake, Leoni. That shit stays with you. If you're on the other side of the phone call, of the knock on the door. That shit stays." She pressed her teeth tight, unblinking, staring at her Italian partner. "It stays, get it?"

He sighed softly. "I can't ask my friend to do that. Not an unregistered flight."

She felt her throat constrict, felt a sudden urge to shout. Didn't he get it? Someone's life was on the line!

He looked at her, though, and with heavy eyes, said, "I know that it stays with you." He nodded once, and for a moment, there was a crack in his calm, placid facade. His eyes blazed with something dark, something hidden deep. He wiped at his sweaty brow, pushing back the single Superman curl of dark hair over his eyebrows. She remembered how he'd been raised by his mother. His story about his father.

"I know you know," she said, urgently. "You get it. Probably better than anyone else. Which means you know we have to try. We *have* to."

He breathed. "I can fly."

She blinked in the dark.

He nodded. "I don't have my license yet. But I've taken enough lessons. I can get us to Germany."

Her mouth unhinged, staring at Leoni. She muttered, more to herself than him... "Of course you can fly... Wouldn't expect anything less from James Bond."

His eyes still flashed, but he grunted once. "Careful with that talk." He turned and began stalking away. "With James Bond, the girls always end up dead."

Adele took off after her Italian partner, a skip in her step. Flying without his license, on an unregistered flight, against the direct orders of their supervisors, this only ended one of two ways. If they stopped the killer, perhaps—*perhaps*—a chance at forgiveness. But if she was wrong again. Wrong a second time...

Losing their jobs would be the least of their worries. She was gambling it all, and now she'd dragged Leoni into the bet with her. But at the end of the day, Adele's job wasn't to please Ms. Jayne. Nor

Executive Foucault. Adele's job wasn't to make Leoni's decisions.

She had only one task: catching killers before they murdered again. She stalked away from Stonehenge, not looking back. It was just a stupid pile of rocks. She followed Leoni, leaving the site and heading back toward where the squad car was waiting. After a few steps, she broke into a jog.

Leoni, in his suit, followed and, side by side, they ran through the night, across the open flatland, toward the distant row of squat, shriveled trees where they'd parked, racing against the clock to catch a killer.

CHAPTER TWENTY SIX

The plane shook for the second time in the last hour, rattling, and a couple of lights flashed on the dash. Leoni's friend had, reluctantly, allowed him to borrow the plane, but Adele was starting to wonder exactly how many lessons he'd taken.

"Are we good?" she asked, sitting in the cockpit this time, her eyes peering through the glass before her as clouds zipped past, little more than patches of dark like oil spills in the night.

"We're good," Leoni snapped, gritting his teeth.

She'd never seen him this flustered before, but at least he'd managed to take off. And, for the last half hour, they hadn't crashed.

"Damn turbulence," he said. "It's fine."

The plane rattled again. "Part of catching this guy requires we get to Germany in one piece."

"I know!" he snapped.

Adele leaned back, double-checking her buckle across her chest. Not that it would matter if they careened from the sky in a flaming heap of scalding metal. But sometimes the small things brought a level of comfort.

Leoni finagled with one of the glinting lights on the dash, and Adele looked away, worrying at her lip.

Then her phone began to ring. Her plane, her rules. She'd just apologize to any flight instruments later.

She felt her phone buzzing against her thigh and every part of her wanted to leave it there, ignoring it. It was an hour before midnight now, which meant whoever was calling her knew she wasn't asleep. Not a good sign.

But another rattle shook the plane and this time Leoni actually cursed, growling toward the nose of the infernal tin can hurtling through the sky.

If only to distract herself, Adele snagged her phone from her pocket, lifting it. "What?" she snapped.

For a moment, there came a stunned silence. Then, a single smack of someone's lips, as if before a sudden tide of words. Adele, despite herself, recognized the sound alone. A flicker of fear whirled through her and her forehead felt very hot all of a sudden.

"Er, Ms. Jayne," she said, quickly. "Sorry. Umm, sorry. I thought you were someone else."

The voice on the other end of the line wasn't so crisp, wasn't so clear as usual. The words almost seemed to jumble together as the correspondent for Interpol said, "What the hell do you think you're doing, Agent Sharp?"

Adele winced. She half glanced through the window, despite herself, partly expecting a drone or a jet to be flying alongside them. But there was no such company. Their plane continued to rattle.

Maybe she was just guessing. "Excuse me?" Adele said.

"Don't you 'excuse me,'" Ms. Jayne roared, all semblance of the calm, collected administrator fading to be replaced by the growl of a lioness. "What do you think you're doing in that plane?"

Adele blinked. So she did know. Shit.

"Agent Sharp! Land that plane, right now!"

Adele gnawed her lip, glancing nervously toward Leoni, who was still battling with the controls and the flashing lights. The airplane rattled again, and Adele nearly bit her tongue.

"Ms. Jayne," she said, starting a sentence she didn't know how to end. "...I...I know I'm right about this," she said at last. "I need you to trust me."

The voice on the other end of the line increased in volume. "Land the plane, now! At this point, you will both be fortunate if you have jobs, no less your freedom after you disembark. German authorities are already asking why an unscheduled flight with two foreign agents is heading into their territory."

"They know?"

"Adele, land!"

For a moment, Adele considered the command. She knew if she wasn't careful, she would be jeopardizing not only her career, her livelihood, but Leoni's as well; on the other hand, she knew she had to trust her instincts. She knew the cost of failing. The tourist in France, the security guard in Greece, the American at the Vatican—these weren't just statistics to her. They weren't just bodies to be forgotten and cases to be managed. These victims, not just these, but all her cases were mothers, fathers, brothers, sisters, children. They were loved ones. And when they were snatched from the world, they left a gap so large, that it felt like it might swallow a person whole. Adele didn't know how to manage such a gap. She didn't know if it *could be* managed. And so she did the only thing she knew how. She stopped the bullet before it was fired.

That was her job. The bureaucrats and Interpol, the agency heads might have other things to worry about. She didn't blame them. It was likely a nightmare to deal with the politics of managing agents across continents. But that didn't change her job. And it didn't change what she needed to do.

"I'm sorry," Adele said. "I know he's going to be there."

"Adele—Adele, don't you dare—"

Adele hung up.

For a moment, she sat in the cockpit next to Leoni, breathing shallow breaths and trying to calm herself. Her chest prickled with pins and needles, and her face felt hot all of a sudden. She had just hung up on the correspondent for Interpol. She had just sealed her fate. Unless...

Unless she was right. Unless she could prove it was worth it.

Do or die.

"Are you all right?" she said, glancing at Leoni.

The plane seem to steady, at least a little. Adele didn't know much about flying, but it seemed like he had lifted them a bit out of the clouds, away from the rattling wind currents. "Fine," he said, curtly, his tongue tucked inside his cheek in concentration.

"They're mad at us," Adele said.

Leoni didn't glance at her, his eyes fixed ahead, through the windshield, down the cone shape of the plane. "My left pocket has been buzzing since we took off. My own agency has been trying to reach me too."

"And you're good with that?"

Leoni finally did glance over at her, and shrugged one shoulder, but then quickly looked back, his fingers gripping the controls firmly. "I have to be," he said.

Adele gnawed on her lip, her mind fizzing and spinning. Thoughts bubbled to the surface, always anxious, always nerve-racking. She needed to focus, but what would that help now? It was a zero-sum game. She was all in on black. The roulette wheel was spinning. Even now, the small white ball bounced around the tumbling wheel, eyes fixated, emotions high, a crowd of onlookers staring, holding their breaths.

She was all in.

Her phone began to buzz again. She glanced down. It was Executive Foucault.

"Who is that?" Leoni asked.

Adele hung up without answering. "No one, just fly."

CHAPTER TWENTY SEVEN

Round hands... round eyes... Around and around and around. The wooden columns circled more wooden columns, circled a fence intent on holding back onlookers...

It wasn't that he had forgotten how to smile, but rather that he reserved the expression for suitable instances. And now, under the cover of darkness, beneath the smile of the midnight moon, he allowed his own lips to twist up at the sides. The rocky ground around him was strewn with old, shattered fragments of stone and splinters of calcified lumber. He moved, slowly, one foot in front of the other, the black duffel bag slung over his shoulder. His supplies needed to be within quick reach.

He spotted a huddled group of figures up against the first ring. Many rings of wood, some stone from reconstruction, some protruding, some gouged into the earth. He watched as one of the figures tossed a glass bottle over their shoulder, and it shattered against one of the logs.

He breathed slowly, allowing the anger to swirl through his gut. There were four of them, college-age, perhaps. Maybe a bit older. It had been a long time since he had been so young. He didn't prefer their company. Stupid, vapid, inane. Just like the rest of this stiff-necked generation.

He hefted the bag again, his eyes flicking toward where the group bunched. They'd spotted him a few minutes ago and perked up, likely guessing he was a cop sent to chase them off. But when he made no move toward them, they'd started laughing, drinking more. After a bit, a couple of them had tried to toss stones at him.

Now, he was out of reach, watching from behind the precipice of lumber. Watching the four figures, potential offerings each one.

"What are you looking at, you stupid hobo?" shouted one of the voices.

The man didn't reply. Of course, he knew German perfectly. But he didn't like to speak to the prey. The offering couldn't be sullied with words, but baptized in action. Baptized in blood.

The figure who was still leaning against one of the wooden columns

145

hefted one of the bottles now, throwing it toward him. "Buzz off," they shouted.

The man didn't flinch, didn't move. He was a prophet in his mind, and he knew the bottle would miss. It shattered against one of the stones at his feet, the residue of liquid spattered against the ground, but it was difficult to spot where the glass had strewn in the darkness.

A couple of the bottle throwers' friends were chuckling now. He spotted a flicker of orange, a lighter, and then a puff of smoke from a cigarette. He watched as another bottle was shattered against the columns.

Fine. He could feel his anger rising, the bile in the back of his throat threatening to consume. Rage had its place. And so did patience.

If married together, rage and patience made the best of friends.

He hefted the duffel bag again, deciding the supplies likely pegged him as homeless in their minds. But he wasn't homeless. He was a wanderer. Everywhere was his home. Especially places like this.

Their feet were like twigs, skeletal feet, with many bones now resting on the ground. What they didn't know was how many bones had once been *beneath* this earth. A gift, really. A gift that made life worthwhile. A gift that could seal deep within this earth, the knowledge required.

"What are you staring at?" one of the voices shouted again.

Four of them. Four was too many. But they were stupid. And slow. Eventually, they would split off. Patience was a virtue of a good hunter. And the prophet had patience in spades. While the pack animals were together, he'd wait and watch. But once the mewling lambs wandered off, then the wolf would show its teeth.

His smile faded now, his face bathed in moonlight. And he stepped around the boulders, disappearing into the shadows.

"Shit," said one of the voices. "Where'd the hobo go?"

"Probably to sleep beneath a tree," replied another.

For some reason this declaration was met by a chorus of giggles.

"Want to find him?" someone said.

"Nah, leave him alone," a voice replied. "He's doing no harm."

The giggling stopped for a moment, suggesting perhaps that this comment wasn't a popular one.

The same voice who'd just spoken cleared their throat and said, "Whatever. I've gotta take a leak."

"It's getting cold," said another.

146

"You all go on without me. There's pizza in the fridge back home."

Voices murmured and the sound of scattered stone and clinking bottles arose. The prophet listened as the earlier voice said, "I'll piss behind a tree and catch up with you. Also, front seat is mine—hear me, Bjerg? Mine!"

A spout of grumbling met this declaration, but then the prophet heard the sound of retreating footsteps. Fading murmurs and laughter. He also heard a steady stream of cursing. He glanced around and spotted a single silhouette, moving *away* from the other three now, heading behind one of the large wooden barriers for privacy.

The little lamb had wandered off.

This time, the prophet didn't smile. This wolf's teeth stayed behind steady lips. For now. He hefted his duffel bag and began to move with slow, strolling steps, sliding through the shadows of the old, hallowed ground as he crept up on the separated little lamb.

CHAPTER TWENTY EIGHT

Adele stared, her eyes wide as she peered down at the highway lights flashing by.

"You sure about this?" she asked, her voice strained.

Leoni tucked his tongue inside his cheek and didn't reply. He focused on the highway below.

"I don't see any cars," Adele called out, playing her role as lookout.

Leoni adjusted the plane, lowering even further, and Adele felt her stomach tip as they began to descend closer and closer toward the highway below. Trees and lights flashed by on either side, illuminating the long stretch of road. Adele shivered as they came closer.

"Landing gear is out," Leoni shouted.

Adele didn't realize until she tasted blood that she'd been biting her lip.

Her phone, mercifully, hadn't been ringing. But now, they were careening down, and she could just about see the Pömmelte Henge visible over the hills, an outline illuminated by glowing lights from a backdrop of civilization. Most of the area was cast in darkness. And night inserted itself across the horizon. Adele wanted to scream. But this was the only way. She glanced at her watch; nearly midnight. If the killer was planning to strike, it would be soon. If the killer was here, which she had to believe he was, someone would die within minutes. And so they'd concocted this harebrained plan.

Even now, she couldn't quite remember if it had been Leoni's idea, or hers. Either way, she knew they would pay for it with Ms. Jayne. Not only was it a pilot without a license, steering them on an uncharted flight into another country, but the Italian agent was now bringing the plane down on an open stretch of highway at night, ignoring airports and runways, deciding to use the asphalt of the autobahn as their landing strip.

If this didn't get them in hot water, Adele felt certain their jobs were already forfeited. Which meant, at this point, they were likely going to face prison time.

But now wasn't the time to worry about such things. The decision had already been made. Already, midnight was approaching. The Stonehenge of Germany was within sight; once they landed, if they landed safely, she would be within running distance.

"You sure you know what you're doing?" she demanded.

"Look out for cars," he retorted.

"I don't see any. But you're *sure*?"

"You buckled?"

"Will that help?"

Leoni shook his head once, gritting his teeth and pushing on the controls. "Probably not. Hang on."

She could practically hear Ms. Jayne screaming in her mind, shouting at the top of her lungs at the stupidity of this move. But Adele was beyond turning back. In for a penny, in for a pound.

Besides, every cloud had a silver lining. If they crashed and burned in a fiery explosion of metal and molten plastic, she wouldn't have to face Interpol or DGSI to account for her actions, which seemed wilder and wilder with each passing moment.

And then her stomach leapt up. The plane tipped down. Finally, she saw the lights on either side whipping by the small eight-passenger plane. She wanted to scream. In a flicker, she spotted an old truck, lights blaring, buzzing toward them.

"Look out!" she screamed.

But Leoni shook his head. "Other lane," he retorted.

A second later, she realized he was right. The truck was going by in the opposite direction, heading along the stretch of road past the concrete divide. At least, mercifully, at midnight, the highways seemed mostly clear.

The lights flashed by through the windows, illuminating the inside of the cockpit, and stretching shadows across her sweat-slicked hands which gripped in front of her lap. Adele tried to hold back a scream. But a small little yelp escaped her lips as the wheels hit the asphalt below.

Leoni loosed a hearty curse. The plane jolted, and for a moment, Adele felt certain he had brought them in too hard.

But Adele watched as Leoni pulled sharply on the controls. After a second, a bounce, another bounce, a loud squeak of skating wheels, they began to slow down.

Still, they weren't safe yet. No trucks coming toward them, no vehicles visible. But the stretch of highway was quickly losing ground.

Ahead, there was a sharp turn. They'd left it too late. The plane barreled toward the turn, and Adele this time couldn't hold back a scream.

For his part, Leoni had turned pale, his knuckles the same color as his cheeks. He gripped the controls, guiding the plane, and she heard a horrible screech of metal. The flaps on the wings, she guessed. She hoped they hadn't lost one. They began to slow, skating beneath the safety lights on either side of the highway, a worrying procession of white streaks of paint beneath the front of the cone-shaped nose. The plane continued to slow. Trees on either side. The Pömmelte was invisible now, out of sight. But Adele, despite herself, tried to keep track of its location in her mind. It wasn't like there was anything else for her to do. It helped her focus, and keep her mind off the horrible, imminent threat of being burned alive.

The plane rushed forward, heading straight toward the curving metal banister.

"Leoni," she shouted.

"I see it," he retorted.

The squeaking sound continued, the plane continued to slip. They weren't going to make it. They would slam into the barrier. Adele winced, bracing herself, her hands rising in front of her, crisscrossing instinctively before her face. She smelled asphalt and burning metal.

But Leoni leaned on the controls and twisted; the plane slowed, slowed, and it was about to hit, but not so fast anymore.

And then the plane shifted; Leoni dropped one of the flaps. It was the only explanation. The plane turned, not sharply, but glacially slow like a corkscrew. Leoni seemed to have overestimated, and the plane wheeled about, nearly falling off the other side of the road. One wing jutted sharply out over the top of the metal banister curving the road. Another crushed into a tree branch, knocking boughs loose.

And then, mercifully, they came to a jarring halt, both of them gasping, sweat on their brows, sitting in a borrowed airplane on a highway in Germany at midnight.

"Holy shit," Adele said, gasping, her chest heaving up and down. She turned, staring at Leoni, and, also breathing heavily, he looked back, shaking his head from side to side. "Never," he said, gasping, "let me," he continued, still puffing air, "do that again."

Adele made a crossing motion over her heart, kissed her fingers, and said, "I won't. I promise."

And for a moment, Adele forgot why they were there. She forgot the fear, forgot the task ahead, forgot the ticking clock, the ire of Ms. Jayne. She just sat there, glad, grateful to be alive. So many people were unable to appreciate the small joys of life. People spent their lives worrying about losing something they could never keep. Not forever. She breathed, exhaling, her blonde hair fluffing up over her nose, and her fingers tightened against the hem of her shirt, if only for something to squeeze for comfort.

Leoni reached out and patted her on the shoulder. "I have to stay with the plane," he said. "Make sure no one hits it."

"Fine," she said, snapping back to the moment. "Of course, yes. How do I get out of here?"

Leoni quickly opened the doors, sliding past her and lowering the steps. The extended metal and aluminum stairs tapped against the asphalt of the highway.

Adele heard a loud, screeching horn and glanced back, watching an enormous hauling truck coming to a halt behind the plane, unable to pass.

At least the truck had stopped. She winced. "Good luck."

Leoni nodded. "You too."

Adele's phone was already out in her hand. She took the steps three at a time and stumbled out onto the highway. The lights lining the road illuminated the night, past the edges of trees, in the direction her GPS was taking her. It seemed so dark, so far all of a sudden. But now wasn't the time for cold feet. She would have to off-road it. They had chosen this highway specifically, because it was within running distance of the Pömmelte Henge. Everything was riding on this. Would the killer be there? He had to be.

She could only hope the killer wasn't already finished with his midnight work.

Adele lowered her head, hands at her side, and sprinted, racing, her legs stretching beneath her, rolling with each motion. She felt more at home on the run than she did in France. More at home on the run than she did in Germany. And more at home on the run than she did trapped in her own thoughts. This was how it should be. Running, not just into danger. But to help someone. And, perhaps just as important, to catch a killer before they shattered another life.

She vaulted the cement barricade lining the highway, ducking beneath a branch that had been knocked loose by the wing of the plane.

151

She could hear now, the truck behind them, leaning on its horn, and another car quickly pulling up, screeching to a halt and slamming on its horn as well. Leoni would have to deal with the locals. Eventually the police would come. It was up to Adele, though, to catch the killer. And so she sprinted, racing through the edge of the forest, away from the autobahn, glancing down at her phone. Every couple of minutes, studying the GPS. The phone estimated it would take her at least fifteen minutes to reach the old wooden and stone burial grounds.

Was fifteen minutes too long? She had to make it ten.

Adele growled, memorizing the path by glancing at her phone once more, then jamming the device in her pocket to free her hand and break into an extra surge of speed, racing over scattered twigs and detritus, racing through trails and switchbacks, moving closer, closer, to the burial ground of druids.

**

Gasping, gun in hand, Adele emerged over the top of the trail. She had seen signs of an old car parked at the bottom of the hill, but the moment they'd spotted her, the driver had careened away. She spotted three forms in the vehicle, and where they had been parked, a scattering of cigarette butts and green bottles littered the ground.

She raced up the hill, toward the outline of stone behemoths beneath the moon. Ancient, echoing, unyielding wood, circling, standing sentry, obstinate and obsolete, forgotten, and yet memorable. Not just a single ring of stone, like the henge in England, but multiple, different-colored wooden barricades circling.

Gasping from her sprint from the highway, her gun in her hand waving in front of her, Adele stumbled through the gaps, into the circle of wood. Then she pulled up short.

It took her a moment, panting at the ground, to adjust.

Then she saw them, like shrouds rising from a deep nightmare, impossible to believe even when confronted with the spectacle.

A figure was standing directly opposite her with a rope tight in his hands. A second, smaller figure was struggling weakly, his fingers scrambling at a noose wrapped around his neck.

Adele felt a surge of vindication. She'd been right. But the thought was quickly replaced by the horror of the moment.

"Drop the rope or I'll shoot," she shouted.

152

The figure holding the rope turned sharply, staring, eyes pale, pulsing in the dark. But instead of complying, he moved, spinning around the side of a wooden archway. For a moment, she issued a gasp of relief. The victim was still alive. But the attacker didn't release the rope. He was behind the wooden barricade, sheltered from her gunfire, and then began to pull, *hard*.

Adele heard the sound of creaking wheels, a jury-rigged pulley system of some sort, and the rope went taut. The small form of the sandy-haired victim, with bulging eyes, was gasping, kicking, and began to be lifted off the ground, the rope tightening around his neck. A quiet scream seemed to rise from his lips, but was suddenly cut short like a speaker dropped into the ocean. He was pulled higher, higher, tugged up, his head banging against the tall column of wood behind him.

"Stop!" Adele shouted. She fired a gunshot into the air, if only to distract the killer.

But he seemed to realize he was out of her line of sight. He didn't falter. He continued to yank the rope; there was the sound of grating wheels as the pulley system did its work, and the rope strained against the victim's neck.

Who was the victim? It didn't matter. The killer had to be stopped.

Desperately, she sprinted around the wood and stone columns, gun raised, trying to get a good angle on the man.

She pulled up short, standing nearly twenty feet away from the fellow gripping the rope; the killer had a wide, unblinking gaze. His hair was wild, frayed, like pictures of Einstein she'd once seen. He was wearing gloves, which wrapped tightly around the rope.

"Drop it!" she snapped.

The killer just stared at her. She didn't recognize his face, and he didn't wear a mask. He had a small, silver goatee. A weak chin, but especially intelligent eyes. She could tell the way he was looking at her that he was already calculating, thinking through his next step.

"Drop it or I'll shoot," she screamed.

But the killer stared at her over the rope and made no move to comply. He didn't speak, but instead inclined his head in sort of coy little nod.

She turned to look, and realized the victim was struggling at the very top of the tall wooden joist. Nearly twenty-five feet in the air.

"Shoot me," he said, his voice soft like velvet, "and he'll break every bone in his body."

"Lower him, now!" Adele screamed.

The killer looked at her, and it took her a moment to realize the reflection of his eyes was actually from glasses. The glass had no frame that she could see, and the thin veneer of corrective lenses seemed to shield his gaze as if beneath a layer of water.

"I can't do that," he said, softly. He shook his head and made a quiet tutting sound. He didn't seem scared at all. In fact, his hands were steady as tombstones. His eyes fixed on her like a gargoyle statue.

"You will be shot dead," she snapped. "You get it? This is over. Lower him!"

The killer didn't respond in kind. Usually, they would. The more shouting, the more they felt the need to increase their own volume. This was tactical. It sometimes would help distract the suspect. But the killer seemed wise to the move. He kept his tone calm, considered. "This has to be done," he said, quietly. "Agent Sharp."

She felt a shiver up her spine. She gazed at him, staring now, also unblinking. "You know who I am?" She glanced up again toward the struggling form of the victim. At least they were still moving. Hands still struggling against the rope. Their neck would snap. But there wasn't much time. They were choking, dying beneath the makeshift gallows. She had to figure out something. She took a tentative step forward, but the killer clicked his tongue. "Don't."

She paused.

"I do know you. I know your name. I checked your work. I try to keep apprised of those who hunt me."

"I didn't know my name was in a newspaper," she said, gritting her teeth.

He smiled at her and shook his head. "Not all information is found in papers."

She wasn't sure what the hell that meant. How did he know her name? She felt a bad taste in her mouth. But that wasn't important. There were ways to bribe, pay people off, create unwitting, or witting, contacts on the force. These things all cycled through her mind. But none of them mattered just yet. What mattered was the gasping, struggling form of the young man being choked to death twenty-five feet in the air. If she shot the killer, the rope would slip and the fellow would fall, breaking his legs and spine. But if she didn't, he would choke, suffocating, gasping, with her helplessly below, staring down

154

the barrel of her gun.

"You think you're clever," she said, breathing heavily. "You know my name. And you think that makes you clever."

But he didn't rise to this bait either. "Agent, is that the best you have? Attack my ego? Try to get me emotional? Distract me. You don't understand what's happening here. I don't blame you. Only one soul must mark the soil. You comprehend this?" He smiled. His teeth reflected like pearls beneath the moon. The sheen of his glasses also flickered back the stars. For a moment, his shadow almost seemed to lengthen, stretching to the base of the rock. He stood firm, his hands steady. Even though the weight must've been heavy, he didn't seem strained by holding the rope.

"No," she said, softly. She edged her tongue between her lips, trying to focus, trying to find an angle. She couldn't shoot. She took another couple steps forward.

But this time, the man snapped, "Don't. One more step, he dies. You have my word. And I won't lie."

"Lying, lying is bad to you, but killing isn't?" Adele asked.

She needed to keep him talking, focused on her instead of his victim. Already, she could see the movements from on top of the column fading, legs kicking, feet falling still, even fingers dropping off the edge of the rope; she was running out of time.

"You don't understand anything," he said.

"You said that a few times. Help educate me."

He shook his head. "The soil needs blood. And no, I don't lie. Lying is for these sheep." He shook the rope, and there was a rattling sound of the pulley, which she realized was lashed around the top of the wooden gallows. Secured in place by what looked like rock-climbing gear.

"All right," she said, "the sheep are the liars. What do you mean by that?"

Now that she was asking him, she hoped he'd relish the chance to educate her. Clearly, his mind was his ego. For a moment, his gaze slipped, glancing off toward the trees, as if gathering his thoughts. She took this opportunity to take another quick two steps forward. This time, he didn't seem to notice. And yet, she had drawn within ten feet of the killer. She could actually see a thin glaze of sweat on his upper lip. She could see his gloves, stretched against the rope itself.

"Everyone has forgotten the gods," he said, softly. "They think they're dead. But they're not. They're dormant. Just look around you.

155

Look at the depravity. Orphans, children, widows, they wail, their teeth gnashing, as they die in the streets of Kolkata, and the cocoa fields of Ghana. You can't even imagine the horrors that I've seen in India, Singapore, Chicago, Los Angeles, New Guinea."

"You're well traveled then," she said.

He smirked at her. "For my job, yes. I built them their buildings. But the structures were built upon piles of bones. Once, they even had me clear out an old cathedral. Had it torn down to make room for a gaudy hotel."

He clicked his tongue. "And then I knew my call. I saw it as clear as day."

Was that before or after you fell on your head? Adele thought to herself. But she kept her eyes open, earnest, interested. Ego. Ego was everything. She had to figure out what to do next. Time was out now. The figure above on the rock had stopped moving. No longer kicking, no longer scrambling. She was out of time. Shit.

The killer kept prattling. "And as the people, the sheep, get fat, line their pockets, desecrate the grounds, they will reawaken the old beasts. Have you heard the weather changing? The next ice age coming? Have you seen the typhoons? The earthquakes? The rumors of war," he said, his voice going low, all of a sudden, into a deep growl.

He shook the rope, and for the first time, his arm seemed to twitch, as of beginning to tremble. He didn't have a plan to get out of this any more than she did. He was improvising. And so was she.

"There's one thing," he said, softly. "I'm not trying to wake the gods. You have to believe me."

"I would never accuse you of such a thing," Adele said.

He seemed to detect some of the sarcasm. "Well, you shouldn't. I'm trying to keep them sleeping. Feeding them, like a mother nurtures its young."

"That's what you are? A mother?"

He grinned at her again. "A wolf bringing back prey to the yapping children."

"These gods? They are your children?"

He hissed now, glaring and growling, spitting off to the side. "You don't understand! I'm trying to save us all. If we wait, the typhoons, the storms, the ice, the earthquakes, the devastation and the plagues. Millions will perish. I'm saving you. You owe me. You don't see it. None of you do. Sheep chasing each other's asses. The smell of your own shit in your nose."

Adele nodded. "Yeah, just a sheep. No one is as smart as you."

He stared at her now, his eyes snapping to her like a cobra zeroing in. "You mock me."

"A little," she said, sidestepping just a bit; now she was within eight feet. Her gun still leveled.

And then she realized her mistake.

She thought she'd been playing his ego. She thought she'd outwitted him, allowing herself to draw near. But the killer had been baiting her too. What she'd taken for a hand twitch had been something else. He had moved his hand, lower down the rope. Lower and closer toward his pocket. Toward his waistband.

And then she realized, with a horrifying sinking sensation, right before she saw him move, that he'd been playing her all along.

His hand darted off the rope and shot toward his hip. She saw the gun a second before the moon caught it, reflecting off the metal. She cursed as he swiveled around with a victorious cry.

And she fired, twice, instinctively.

Two bullets. One hit his arm. The other struck his head.

He went over, stumbling, and to her horror, the rope slipped completely. She tossed her gun to the side. A stupid move. But no time to think. She leapt forward. She didn't have the benefit of gloves. But she managed to get close enough, and she grabbed the rope. She held on, screaming in pain as the rope ripped at her hands. She felt the burn streaking across her fleshy palms, ripping skin, spreading blood.

The rope went taut, her arms jolted, but she allowed herself to be dragged forward, refusing to pull too sharply and do the killer's work for him. For a moment, she felt her elbow pop and her feet scatter dust as she was yanked forward. And she yelled again. But she caught the rope, groaning against the victim's weight and easing the rope down, her feet still following the momentum.

Still, gasping in agony, her hands on fire, she quickly lowered the rope. She felt the weight go slack the moment the victim hit the ground.

Mercifully, she let go of the rope, her hands spread. No posture made them remotely comfortable. The agony spread across her fingers, spread over her palms. She tried to flex her hands, and it just shot another bolt of sheer pain. She tried to hold still, and it was still agony, like dipping an open wound in saltwater.

She heard a groan and glanced over. The victim was twitching,

157

moving. She felt a flutter of relief.

She heard another groan. Her heart leapt in her throat. She turned, and to her astonishment, she saw the killer shifting, trying to sit up. She took a couple of hurried steps over and kicked his gun out of the way. It skittered off behind a wooden column; she spotted a black duffel bag hidden beneath some shrubs. His glasses had fallen off. Blood was pouring down from his head wound. And yet, his eyes were twitching. He was still breathing. Somehow, he had survived a bullet to the skull. Maybe some people just had brains enough to spare. A morbid thought.

Then again, it wasn't like his big brain had gotten him very far.

She tried to reach for her phone and managed to pull it from her pocket, but then screamed from the sheer pain of the rope burns. Her phone dropped, hitting the dust.

She bent over, trying to grasp it, but it felt like someone was jabbing needles all up and down her hands.

A few moments later, though, she heard shouting. She glanced back, tears pouring from her cheeks now. Her hands held out in front of her, like a child begging for food. The victim was struggling, gasping for air. The killer was bleeding from two gunshots, also gasping.

She saw whirring blue and red lights. She heard more shouting, then static from radios. She felt a sudden surge of desperate relief as German police swarmed up the hill, guns raised, moving toward her.

"Adele Sharp," one of them was shouting. "You're under arrest!" he screamed.

For a frustrating moment, she realized they were here for her. Probably due to the airplane causing the traffic jam. Two officers reached her first, with five others following close behind, and they pulled up short. She jerked one of her wounded hands, indicating generally toward the victim and the killer. "That's the Monument Killer," she said, gritting her teeth. "And that guy needs an ambulance." She paused, then shrugged. "They both do."

And then, wincing, satisfied by the astonished looks on the faces of the police, she allowed herself to be put in handcuffs, escorted away from the scene, glad to hear the yammering calls over the radio for ambulances, for EMTs, and for further backup.

She looked at the moon as she was escorted toward the nearest squad car. She spotted Leoni, tucked in the backseat already. He looked out at her. She nodded once.

He smiled and seemed to breathe a sigh of relief. For her part, she looked at the sky again, studying the moon, the stars, and she smiled. She'd been right. She'd saved a life. That's all that mattered.

CHAPTER TWENTY NINE

Adele sat in the cold, sparse, holding cell, yet her thoughts carried more warmth than the bleak gray walls and floor around her. Daylight moved through the ceiling-level window above her. She breathed a gentle sigh toward the concrete, the back of her head resting against the wall where her shoulder blades grazed the rough, unpainted surface. Her left arm hung in a white sling, in a crook near her ribs. She winced a bit, readjusting.

She'd been right. But that didn't mean everyone appreciated the method. Adele could still feel the raw marks around her wrists where the handcuffs had been pressed too tight. Apparently, the German police didn't appreciate private planes being parked on their autobahn.

She heard a *clink*, and then the sound of marching footsteps. Her eyes flicked up, and she spotted one of the arresting German officers moving down the cold corridor to the holding cells.

For a moment, Adele felt a flutter of relief, but then, a second later, her heart plummeted. Behind the officer, Ms. Jayne came walking in like an angel of death appearing in the frame of the door. Adele resisted the urge to bite her tongue. For a moment, she felt like a schoolgirl caught by the principal. She wasn't sure exactly where to look. After a couple of hyperventilated breaths, though, she reminded herself she wasn't a child in need of reprimand.

Her stomach still twisted, and her chest prickled with nerves. At last, she settled on glancing through the iron bars of the holding cell, flicking her gaze down the hall toward Ms. Jayne's approaching form. The German police officer stepped to the side, clicked an electronic lock, and the door to Adele's cell sprang open.

Ms. Jayne approached and came to a halt with one red-shoed foot resting on the line between the cell and the hall, while her other foot slanted off toward the exit.

Adele remained sitting on the bed, but then decided she didn't like how it felt to be looked down on by Ms. Jayne. She got to her feet, shakily, wincing as she pushed off with her free hand, careful not to move the arm in the sling too much. Thankfully, the German police had provided bandages and ibuprofen. Both her hands were wrapped in gauze. She could still feel the heat from where she'd gripped the slipping rope, but the pain wasn't as bad as last night.

"Agent Sharp," said the Interpol correspondent.

Adele winced. "Ms. Jayne."

"Quite a showing."

Adele shrugged. "Saved a life."

"Broke seven international laws as far as I can tell," Ms. Jayne said, her expression impassive. She was a bit heavier than most field agents, with white hair and grandmotherly features. Everything about her seemed neat, clean, contained. Even now, there was no sign of the voice that had been barking at Adele over the phone to land the plane. Ms. Jayne simply peered out from her spectacles, eyeing Adele where she stood in the cell.

"You were right," the Interpol correspondent said at last. "I can't say your methods were particularly conventional, but you were right."

Adele blinked.

"Of course, that doesn't mean you should've disobeyed a direct order."

Adele winced. She rubbed at one of her ears and said, "Honestly, the cell reception was just really bad."

For a moment, Ms. Jayne studied Adele. She seemed to be weighing her options. Specifically, she seemed to be deciding if she was going to let Adele set the narrative. *Bad reception. Hard to hear.* A simple enough lie. Perhaps one that could be repeated. Of course, both of them knew the truth.

At last, eyes still narrowed, Ms. Jayne said, "I've heard that before. Something about the plane's electronics. It would've been unsafe for you to try to call back."

Adele felt a flutter of hope in her chest. "Yeah, that's right. I didn't want to damage the plane."

"Of course, you didn't know you were breaking the law, did you?"

Adele hesitated, mouth half open. She swallowed then and gave a quick shake of her head. "Er. Mm-mm."

The correspondent smiled like a poker player who knew they had the best hand. "Which means you will have to spend at least two weeks in mandatory retraining, brushing up on international flight law."

Adele winced. "Wait, hang on—*two weeks?*"

"Are you saying you *did* know you were breaking international

161

law?"

Adele's countenance fell; she breathed in frustration, but then shook her head. It was a punishment, obvious enough. But a punishment that didn't end behind bars. She'd have to bite the bullet on this one. "Training? And would that be with Interpol?"

An innocent enough question, but with severe implications. Ms. Jayne just looked at Adele and then said, "After retraining, I can't see any reason your capacity should change." Her tone became a little less guarded now, and the older woman half glanced toward the police officer watching them. She sighed and said, "You did a good job there. Adele. The victim is going to make it."

"He's being treated?" Adele said, trying to hide the sudden surge of relief flooding her.

"Yes. At the local hospital. The killer too, on the same floor, in fact. Of course, we have six police officers guarding the madman."

Adele shook her head. "Well, good..." She trailed off and winced. "Does this mean I'm free to go?"

Ms. Jayne glanced at her wrist, checking her watch, and then nodded to the German officer. "Henry here will see you out. I have a meeting with the chief to help smooth things over. Have a good day, Agent Sharp. And I'm serious about that retraining. Two weeks, ten-hour days. Good day."

And then Ms. Jayne turned, marching off, her shoes clicking against the floor, her posture straight, her eyes ahead; not once did she look back.

Adele stared after the older woman, feeling a mixture of emotions, both despair at the thought of two weeks of rookie tests and training and lessons. But also stupefied she still had a job, and wasn't going to be thrown in prison. She gave a small, incredulous shake of her head and breathed a slow sigh of relief.

The German officer gestured toward Adele, and she took her time about leaving the cell, not wanting to catch up with Ms. Jayne. An involuntary shiver jolted through her at the mere thought of trying to maintain a conversation, walking side-by-side with that woman. No, perhaps it was best to linger behind a bit. She kept her arm in the sling close to her side as they moved—her bandaged hands motionless.

The police officer guided Adele out of the holding cell room, toward the front of the precinct. She paused at an old locker room converted into a storage vestibule. Behind bulletproof glass, a frowning

162

woman pushed two plastic baggies toward Adele, followed by a pen and clipboard.

"Verify everything is there," she said in German, "then sign."

After signing with a limp hand, the plastic bags crinkled as Adele delicately retrieved her things, taking back, with one hand, her weapon, her smart watch, wallet, ID cards and then, doing her best to ignore the angry looks from the other police officers in the precinct, she moved toward the front doors and stepped out into free air.

Sunlight streaked the marble steps and gray clouds rolled across the horizon. For a moment, she heard the glass doors swish behind her, as if sealing her back out in the real world, beneath the free skies and gentle wind. She smiled softly to herself, fiddling carefully with the band to her reacquired watch.

"You made it too," said a voice. And she jerked, startled.

She glanced over. The handsome frame of Agent Leoni was silhouetted against the opaque glass window in the far wall of the precinct.

Her nerves quieted again and she said, "When did you get out?"

Leoni rubbed ruefully at his wrists, somehow managing to make this gesture suave and chagrined at the same time. "Only an hour ago."

"Prognosis?"

"I'm on warning. Two weeks. Unpaid suspension."

Adele whistled. "Sorry."

Leoni shook his head. "I was expecting much worse. It sounded like someone from Interpol want to bat for *you*, which meant I got some second-hand goodwill. Two weeks, I can deal with that."

Adele moved to cross her arms on instinct, but then winced at her sprained elbow and burned hands. "You waited for an hour?"

He smiled now, his cheeks splitting. "That's what you took from all that?"

Adele studied Leoni, her eyes slipping along his dark gaze, down the smooth slant of his jaw, to his perfectly maintained teeth. But he didn't just look it, he actually *was* handsome. He had proven himself loyal, willing to risk himself and his career to save a life. She nodded at him once. "I have to go. Flight back to France."

"You still have a job?"

"Two weeks of retraining. International flight law."

Leoni winced. "Wow, I got it better."

"No kidding. Two-week vacation? What I wouldn't give."

They both chuckled at this. Adele gave Leoni a nod which he returned, and then she began to move away toward the curb, fishing out her phone with gentle motions to call a cab. After a bit though, she paused, standing on the sidewalk, and glanced back. Leoni was sitting on the bench now, glancing at his watch, likely waiting for his own ride. She called, her voice echoing up the precinct steps, "If ever you're in Paris, you should stop by."

Leoni's dark eyes flicked up and studied her for a moment where he sat on the bench. He brushed his Superman curl out of his eyes. It struck Adele as incredible that somehow his suit was still unwrinkled. "I'd like that," he replied.

She turned back to the road, smiling now, and scheduling her cab.

***

This flight involved far less adrenaline or screaming bosses, and Adele was glad to be back in first class, rather than the cockpit. She was additionally glad to be leaning as far back as her chair would go, thanks to the empty seat behind her. No work this time. No laptop, or case files, or anything. If she wanted, she could watch a movie or, as she was doing now, take a nap. She pulled her blanket up beneath her chin, nestling into the seats, her window shade half closed, allowing light to stream through, warm against her cheek. The cool air from the nozzle above her intermingled with the warmth from the sun, and she felt like a cat in a sunbeam. Content.

But, though her eyes were closed, and though she had an opportunity for rest, it was a difficult thing to turn off the mind of an agent.

It all came back to Adele's mother. But perhaps that was why she'd been failing to catch the killer back in Paris. Why she had failed ten years ago. And why the Spade Killer, as the news had called him, had escaped.

Because it *shouldn't* all trace back to Elise.

In fact, in the killer's mind, Elise was just a tool, a plaything. In the killer's mind, it all went back to him.

This new psycho had reminded her of that. She had thought like a killer because she knew killers. That was how she was able to catch him. That was how she was always able to catch them. Every case, it was the advantage she had. She thought of herself like a bloodhound

164

with a scent. But that scent was a knowledge. The scent was her ability to put herself in the minds of these monsters.

And yet with her mother, she hadn't managed to. She'd been putting herself in the mind of her mother. Queue the dreams, the horror, the nightmares. Queue the sympathy, the empathy, the tears.

But an investigator couldn't risk those things. She wasn't trying to figure out Elise's thoughts. She knew her mother and it was useless for the case.

She needed to figure out the killer. Which meant she had to put aside, for a moment, the memories of her mother. Put aside empathy for the woman who'd been taken. And embrace fully knowledge, empathy, understanding of the murderer who'd sliced up innocent women, leaving them to die, bleeding out on the side of a park path.

Perhaps, an impossible thing. But empathy could be turned off as well as on. She needed to find the murderer. Which meant she needed to think like him. She'd been playing it too safe, and playing it too emotional. She'd been letting her feelings cloud her judgment.

She knew she had to get into the killer's head and understand his unique and bizarre view of the world if she was ever going to catch him. And while it felt like a betrayal to her mother, to think of that case in terms of anything but Elise's own story, she knew the killer cast himself as the main character. Which meant she would have to as well.

And though it was an unsettling thought, Adele felt a tranquility descend on her as she lay back in that airplane seat. Her eyes were closed, and she didn't smile, but she didn't frown. She dreamed. It was as sleep came, the nightmares returned.

But for the first time ever, *bleeding, bleeding, always bleeding*, as she watched the images flash through her mind, she viewed them not from her mother's perspective, not from her own perspective, but from the eyes of someone standing off the side of the road, amidst the trees, studying the death, the carnage, studying the work of art he'd left for others to find.

In this place, with her mind engaged, she heard a quiet buzz. She frowned, glancing at her phone connected to the plane's Wi-Fi.

A message from John.

It read: *We need to talk. ASAP.*

CHAPTER THIRTY

Adele took the stairs up to her apartment with a slight spring to her step, as if she were shedding a burden at the base of the hall. She no longer wore the sling, and though her elbow still throbbed occasionally, she did her best not to move it. Even the discomfort from her injuries couldn't dampen her thrill of excitement as she curled around the banister of the old building and moved higher and higher. No elevator, which suited Adele just fine. Her hands were hurt, not her legs. She liked the required exertion, like built-in exercise to her own home.

She was back in Paris. She'd only received a slap on the wrist for the events back in Germany, but Adele didn't care about any of it just now.

She could still feel the cool metal of her phone through the lining of her pocket. The same phone that had carried a message from Agent Renee. What was so urgent? *ASAP,* he'd said. Something in the case?

She had told him she needed space. Told him to leave her alone. But now, he wanted to talk. He'd asked when she would be home, and if she would meet with him back at her place.

Adele took the stairs three at a time. Her legs stretching pleasurably as she reached her floor. Her handbag carry-on swayed next to her, where it dangled loosely from her good arm as she moved, and she felt her hair shifting across her sweaty forehead. A night sprinting through forests, another in jail, followed by a flight from Germany... Adele wrinkled her nose at the thought. She needed a shower. She could only hope John wouldn't arrive until after she'd had a chance to settle.

But as she rounded the wooden banister, her luggage and laptop bag dangling from the same arm crook, she pulled up and spotted a tall form outlined against the doorframe of her apartment.

Agent Renee had his arms crossed, his long legs stretched over the hall and pressed to the metal bars of the stairwell.

Her eyes flicked to his face at the same time as his head snapped up.

And for a moment, she stopped, pausing at the top of the stairs, staring at her old partner.

166

John gave a small little fluttering wave with one hand. He had dark features, a sharp, bold nose, and eyes that were always half hooded like a lazy tomcat in a dark alley. A thick scar, from burn marks, roped down his chin over his throat and toward his chest.

He wasn't wearing a suit, but had opted for a ten-dollar hoodie and sweatpants, stained on one sleeve. Anyone else in such attire waiting outside a young woman's apartment would have elicited a call to the cops. Adele wondered if any of her neighbors had asked who he was.

She cleared her throat a bit, adjusted her own shirt with one free, still bandaged hand, absentmindedly brushed a few loose strands of hair behind an ear, and then approached, not quite smiling, but also not frowning.

"Adele," John said as she drew near.

"Renee," she replied.

"Miss me yet?"

"You're the one who texted me."

"Right." His tone went very serious all of a sudden, and Adele paused again, this time standing in front of her own door, next to her old partner. He didn't smell like cologne, but more like sweat, and worry.

A strange aura from John Renee. He wasn't normally a man given to worry. He didn't seem to think too much of the emotion. But now, in his every sidelong glance and twist of his heel against the ground, Adele discerned something lurking there. Something uncomfortable.

"How can I help you?" Adele said.

John snorted. He reached out and put a finger against her chin, not too hard, but firm enough so he could guide her to look him in the eyes.

She reached up and slapped his hand away.

"How can you *help me*? What is this, a bank?"

Adele, now that she was looking at him, refused to look away lest he take it as a sign of weakness. She wasn't even sure what she was feeling. She'd been excited, almost like a schoolgirl, at the thought of meeting her partner again. But when she'd seen him, something else had snapped in place. Some other, deeper emotion. One of rejection? Embarrassment? Vulnerability?

She had run from Paris. Run from the killer who had targeted her own mother. She'd abandoned the case to John. It wasn't his fault. It was hers. And yet she couldn't bear being around it. He must think she was so pathetic. Such a coward.

167

The thoughts burned through her mind, and robbed the last vestiges of any attempted smile. Now, she felt alone, her shoulders shaking. With a slight sigh, she tore her gaze away, fished the key from her pocket, and began prodding it toward the locked door to her apartment. She winced a couple of times as her numbed fingers and palm encased in the bandages from the rope burns made it difficult to navigate the lock.

"Look," he said, sternly. "We need to talk."

"About what?" she grunted. "The case?"

"Exactly."

"We landed a plane on a highway, and I grabbed a rope before the victim fell. Big deal."

John snorted in frustration. "I'm not talking about your case. I'm talking about—"

"I know what you're talking about."

John blinked. "So you heard?"

Adele pushed open her unlocked door and stepped into her apartment. She glanced around; everything was the way it had been left. Neat, tidy, save a cereal bowl near the sink.

She sighed, shouldering her laptop bag and luggage carry-on where they had slid uncomfortably close to her hand. She moved into the small apartment. John waited at the threshold of the door, shifting uncertainly. Adele didn't invite him in. She'd let him figure that one out on his own.

"Adele, how much did you hear?" John said, his voice extending from the doorway as she came to a stop by the island counter. Across from her small kitchenette.

"About your case? Nothing. I haven't been kept apprised."

John went suddenly still. His eyes narrowed. "Wait, so you don't know."

"I don't know anything. And honestly, John, while I'd love to hear what you found, I need a shower, some sleep,"

"I saw the killer."

Whatever she'd been expecting to hear, it wasn't this.

Adele just blinked at him, and she found the strap to her laptop bag slid suddenly down her shoulder, and her fingers went numb, painful beneath their bandages. The bag thudded to the hardwood floor. She stood feet at shoulder width, inhaling softly through her nose. She detected the faint smell of cinnamon, from one of those unlit scent candles on the kitchen table.

"Hang on, what do you mean?"

John still stood in the doorway, but he stretched his frame. Now, his arms reached up, past the doorframe on his side of the hall; he rested his fingers against the wall above the door.

"I mean, I saw the killer. He was torturing a victim. I got there just in time."

"Why didn't you call me?"

"I did. Just now. You said you wanted to be left alone."

"Forget about that. You saw my mother's killer?"

John's hands dropped from above the door now, and he held them up in mock surrender. "Hang on," he said, quickly. "No one said anything about it being your mother's killer. We don't know that yet."

Adele's second bag thumped on top of the laptop bag, and she crossed her arms now, staring at John, who looked at ease in his old hoodie and sweatpants.

"Copycat killer?" Adele snorted. "Are you guys still going with that? Please. Attacking a woman with the same middle name as my mother? After I started poking around? What are the odds, John? Really?"

John shrugged.

Adele huffed. "How did you see them? Did you get a good look at them?"

He winced. "I got a good look. They were wearing a mask. But, before they saw me, the mask was lowered. I got a look. Not long."

"What did you see?" Adele said, her heart pulsing and her face warming, leaving tingles across her cheeks. She wouldn't have been surprised if her face had gone completely pale.

"Clean-shaven. I couldn't tell his age. Pale skinned. Also small, like a small skeleton—couldn't have been much larger than a child. Something off about one of his eyes. But I didn't get a good enough look. The killer saw me coming."

"You chased him?"

John hesitated.

"Dammit, are you saying he got away?" Adele gritted her teeth. She could feel anger surging through her. Now, some of it irrationally directed at her old partner. "John, tell me you at least got a license plate. Something?"

John was now the one no longer making eye contact. He glanced at the ground and rubbed sheepishly at his chin. "I," he said, stuttering, "I didn't chase him. I couldn't. His victim was bleeding out on a table. I had to choose."

"You let the killer get away?"

Now, though, even though he was still just standing in the threshold of the doorway, John's voice rose as well. "Yes," he snapped. "I let the killer get away. To save his victim. And I did. Mr. Maldonado's going to make a recovery. I did that."

Adele stared, firm, her eyes unyielding. "That's a lot of credit for one person. You know how much work I put into trying to find this bastard? Years. Years of my life! And you had him within shooting distance, and you let him get away!"

"It wasn't like that."

"It sure sounds like it. Dammit, John, why?"

John was gritting his teeth so hard, Adele felt she heard one pop. John rubbed at his chin, and he said, "Honestly, I thought you'd be happy. Happy that I got a glimpse, and I'll be working with a composite artist. We might be able to figure out something more from that."

Adele breathed softly, trying to focus. She closed her eyes for a moment, shaking her head slowly. Was it really John's fault, or was she just taking her frustrations out on him? She breathed again, calming herself, and then said, "Sorry. No, really. Look, sorry—I'm lashing out. It wasn't your fault. You did a good job."

John nodded once, carefully, as if waiting for the other shoe to fall.

But Adele just shook her head morosely and closed her eyes against a sudden headache. "Look," she said. "You did the right thing. I get that. I'm happy to help in any way. Just tell me what I need to do."

She opened her eyes, looking at her partner now. At her own words, she could feel anxiety rising again, but she'd already made her peace. Now, it wasn't about her mother. It wasn't about Adele. It was about catching the murderer.

John crossed his arms now too. The tall, lean, dark-featured agent, who reminded Adele of a James Bond villain, stared across the small apartment, toward his tired, iron-willed counterpart. He frowned for a moment, and nibbled the corner of his lip. Their eyes met, and neither of them seemed like they wanted to look away.

"Christ, Adele," John said, slowly. "I wasn't looking to start anything with you. But I don't want you on the case."

She stared blankly. "Wait, what?"

"I don't want you on this case," he repeated, more firmly now. "You're not thinking straight. Hell, I appreciate the apology, but a minute ago you were nearly asking me to let a victim bleed out." He shook his head. "No. Take a break—get some rest. I thought... I thought maybe you'd be ready, but you're clearly not."

She stared at him now, her pulse quickening. "John, this is my case... You know what—"

"It means a lot to you. But actually, it's my case. And you're not thinking straight. No. I'm sorry. Really."

"Damn it, John!" she snapped. "You don't get to make that call."

"I do. Foucault gave me a wide berth. We talked about this before I even started. He says I know you best—says I can make the call. Well, I'm making it. You're out."

Her temper swelled in her like ash against the crumbling seal of a volcano. "John, don't be insane," she snapped. "I have to help on this one. You know I do!"

"Not now. Not yet. You're too emotional."

"Damn right I'm emotional! The psycho killed my mother! John, be reasonable!"

But her partner shook his head adamantly now, crossing his own arms.

She looked at him, and saw beneath it all an expression of frustration and hurt. Though, the second part he'd mastered at concealing over many years, and only someone close to him could detect it in the tightening of his jaw and the flash of his eyes. Adele faltered at this, breathing slowly, trying to push aside the sudden swarm of fury in her chest.

For a moment, she took stock of her own emotions. She cycled through the thoughts hounding her, trying to focus, trying to justify the way she was reacting. And then it settled in her, like a mantle on her shoulders.

She was jealous.

She wasn't sure why she was jealous. She didn't want to be jealous. But she was jealous.

Jealous that after all these years of searching, John had taken one crack at the case and gotten further than she ever had. Who was he to tell her she was out?

As the thoughts dawned on her, her eyes narrowed, and she wanted to punch something. John seemed to sense her discontentment, and

171

though she was no longer looking at him, his voice probed into the still, dark apartment.

"I'm not the enemy here," he said. "I'm closer than we've been."

"I'm closer," she snapped. "*I* am. My case. My mother."

She looked at John again, and this time, found no signs of the hurt from before. As often was the case with men like John, the hurt had very quickly gone through a chemical transformation into sheer anger. "Your case? If it was your case, you would've had a chance to save a life or chase the killer. I chose to save a life. It's my case—and that's it. No discussion."

"You should've done both."

"There was no way," John retorted. "Besides, who are you to lecture me?" he said, going on the offensive for a change. John Renee wasn't the sort of man to cower in a corner for long. "You mock the way I work, but you weren't even here. You ran off hiding, like an ostrich with its head in the sand. You were too scared to do what I did."

She pressed her lips tightly together. "Watch it," she snapped.

But he shook his head once. "I came here to keep you in the loop. I'm starting to realize that was a bad call. I'll remind you, Agent Sharp," he said, a sneer to these words, "you're the one who told me to back off. You're the one who told me you wanted distance. I tried to solve this case for you. Because I knew how much it meant for you. But when it comes down to it, when push comes to shove, I'm going to do my job. And my job does not require me to sacrifice innocent victims in order to please the great Adele Sharp. If you can't understand that, you're not even half the person I thought you were."

"You self-righteous—" Adele began, feeling her own anger bubbling up, but John was gone. The doorway remained open, revealing the stairwell beyond. After a moment, frowning, her blood boiling, Adele heard the sound of John's footsteps, thumping against the stairs as he retreated, leaving her alone in her apartment.

Good riddance. John didn't have what it took. He'd let the killer get away. He betrayed the memory of her own mother. But as these thoughts cycled, Adele felt how weak and flimsy they were to the test. John had been trying to help her. He'd wanted to solve the case for her. Besides, wouldn't she have done the same thing? She practically had in the case in Germany. She'd chosen to save a life instead of following protocol. She had chosen to try to save a life instead of pleasing the other agents involved in the case. And he was right in a way—she was

172

too emotional. Maybe she wasn't ready... maybe not yet... So why was it that she was requiring him to do something different?

"Because it was my fucking mother," she muttered to herself.

Adele stomped across the apartment unit, grabbed the door handle to the metal frame, and slammed it shut.

Fingers trembling, she reached into her pocket, not quite certain what she was doing. She stalked over to the window, peering out into the street below. For a moment, she thought she spotted John's tall figure moving up the street toward a parked Cadillac. She looked away, glancing in the opposite direction. With the phone out, ringing now, she waited.

After a second, the voice answered, "Agent Sharp?"

"Leoni," she replied.

For a moment, Adele wondered what on earth she was doing. Adele knew the killer was now alerted. He was on the run and though John may have glimpsed his face for a moment, it would've been in the dark, in an adrenaline-laced situation. She couldn't count on that. And yet, she felt alone. Which, perhaps, was why she was still on the line.

"Adele?" came Leoni's voice. "Is everything okay?"

"Remember what we said today?" she said, slowly. "That you might visit Paris sometime soon? You're on a two-week leave, yeah? What do you think about moving up that date? I could use the company, but I could also use the help on a case."

Bold words. Especially given the short tenure she'd known Leoni. The handsome Italian agent had gone silent on the other end of the line. For a moment, she felt silly, a preemptive rejection. But before she could talk, Leoni said, "Let me check my schedule."

"No worries. You can get back to me—"

"I'm joking. Like I said, suspended. Yeah, I think that should work. What day works best?"

Adele thought of that shower she wanted to grab, but then again, some things had to wait.

"Whatever you want. I'll text you my address. I have a spare room; well, technically it's the living room, but it does have a couch which pulls out into a bed."

"Are you inviting me to spend the night?"

Adele paused for a moment. John be damned. Eventually, he'd see sense. He would have to. Because one way or another, she *was* going to work this case.

She said, "I'm inviting you to come help me catch a killer."

CHAPTER THIRTY ONE

He listened, smiling, half of his mouth angled down, the other half curling up, his eyes fixed on the blank wall over his desk, the phone cradled against his chin.

He listened as Adele and this new man made plans. Another agent by the sound of things.

He crossed his legs in the leather chair. A larger man might not have been able to do so, but he was skin and bones according to some; he didn't mind this description, seeing as he often felt an affinity toward the skeletal. He listened, taking notes as Adele continued to speak to this Agent Leoni. Of course, he'd had her phone tapped not just for months, but years. He'd always found a way. Connections provided opportunity.

He continued to listen, smirking as Adele finally hung up. He would have to check back tomorrow morning, to see if anything new came up.

He reached down, placing the phone back in its cradle, and then rubbed at the back of his hands, wincing as he did. He'd cut his fingers in his attempt to flee that house.

Now, the man's face wrinkled into a frown. He hated doing it. Killing a friend like that. A good friend. A loyal friend.

Loyalty had to be repaid. And yet, he'd been forced to kill the man. Andrew Maldonado, factory worker. Messenger.

He smiled at the thought, moving away from his desk, and moving with slow, purposeful steps toward the room on the opposite side of the long hall. This room had locks, and bolts, and even one chain. From within the room, he could hear noises. Quiet, gentle, mewling noises.

He began to hum to himself as he approached, his mind still spinning.

Mr. Maldonado had helped sneak the messages into the candy bars for Elise to find. He shuddered at the memory of the name. Elise. One of his favorites. A masterpiece that one.

He winced again as his knuckles brushed against the metal door as he undid the chains and locks. His other fingers were splotched in whites and reds and green dyes. Work. His true work. He would have to remember to wipe off before going out again.

Adele didn't know her phone was bugged. They never did. They never suspected just how resourceful he could be. But that's what it took to stay ahead of the game. That's what it took to stay free for more than a decade and a half.

He thought he'd hung up his boots, passed the game onto protégés and younger allies. But now, he was getting the itch. He wanted to play again. And he'd started already. That other girl, the same name as Adele's mother. A message, more than a plaything. A means to an end, rather than a proper work of art.

Adele was also a friend. She didn't know it yet, but they would soon be bound together. Their paths and fates were inextricably linked. He knew that now. He'd been fighting it, like a star-crossed lover lying to their emotions. But there was no denying this anymore. He needed her. He missed her. And soon, they would be together again. For as long as it took.

He unlatched the last bolt on the door and pulled it open, revealing a dark, windowless room within. The sounds from inside had faded now to a quiet whimper, but as he peered into the studio, his half smile returned, once again twisting up the side of his cheek.

He stepped in, closing the door quietly shut behind him. Soon, Adele would be here with him. And soon, they would have so many things to talk about. He couldn't wait.

He leaned in, whispering softly, "And what is his name?"

His voice was higher pitched than people usually guessed, given his appearance. He didn't put on a show, nor did he try to make his voice impressive or needlessly threatening as they did in the TV shows and movies. Serial killers, that's what they were called in film and television; the weak, the powerless, the useless losers of the world—society's fringe—felt a kinship, a bond, a violent, hateful lashing out against the culture that their victim souls saw as oppressive.

But he knew better. He knew that truly powerful people didn't have to playact. Not their words, but their actions gave them that power.

He leaned in even closer now. He had picked up the stray little thing just outside the DGSI building. A hilarious thing to him, how little security was actually kept around the headquarters itself.

"You said she's close to two people. Give me their names."

Her voice warbled and shook, trembling. "Please," she gasped,

176

"please, stop hurting me."

"That is not an option," he said, quietly. "I already told you, you earned yourself three days of pain trying to escape. You're on day two. So there's nothing I can do. I really am sorry. But I will hurt you today and tomorrow. If you answer my questions, though, we won't make it six days. Do you understand?"

He spoke gently, hopefully, as if he were on her side, like a palliative care worker.

The woman tied to the chair, streaked in blood but covered with bandages so she didn't bleed out, was whimpering now and shaking her head.

He lowered his voice, growling, "Two names you said she was close to at that infernal place. Who?"

At last, trembling, the woman's eyes noticed what was happening with his hand. He had picked up one of the scalpels next to the palette on the counter by the low-hanging painting he'd made when he was young. A simple, silly painting of trees and wind and water. But a painting he was proud of. One of the first ones that was any good.

"I don't know, you have to believe me, no, no, don't—" The scalpel descended, and she screamed, protesting. "I'll tell you. No, please. I'll tell you."

He waited, the scalpel just above the exposed flesh of her chest. "Names."

"John Renee," the woman said, gasping. "Adele Sharp was close with John Renee."

But he shook his head, growling. "I know about John. The tall skyscraper. No, he won't do. The other name. Tell me."

The woman whimpered, her eyes shifting to the scalpel and back up to his gaze. Then, swallowing, she said, "Another agent. Older. He's sick. Very sick."

The man smiled and nodded. "Perfect. And what's his name?"

"He was Adele's mentor for years. They're very close."

"What's his name?"

"If I tell you, you have to stop hurting me. Please."

He hurt her. Waited for her screaming to stop, and said, "I already told you. There's nothing I can do. You've earned yourself two days more. Unless you want me to make it six, or twelve, or twenty-four; I'm not in any rush, the record I had once was a full year, every day, inflicting all sorts of interesting things on my friend. Is that what you'd like, dearie?"

A quiet, sobbing whimper burst from the woman's lips, but she violently shook her head side to side at an insistent flick of his now bloodied scalpel.

"Give me a name," he said.

"Robert," she gasped. "Her mentor's name is Robert Henry."

NOW AVAILABLE!

LEFT TO LAPSE
(An Adele Sharp Mystery—Book 7)

"When you think that life cannot get better, Blake Pierce comes up with another masterpiece of thriller and mystery! This book is full of twists and the end brings a surprising revelation. I strongly recommend this book to the permanent library of any reader that enjoys a very well written thriller."
--Books and Movie Reviews, Roberto Mattos (re Almost Gone)

LEFT TO LAPSE is book #7 in a new FBI thriller series by USA Today bestselling author Blake Pierce, whose #1 bestseller Once Gone (Book #1) (a free download) has received over 1,000 five star reviews.

When a body turns up on a high-speed train passing through France, Germany and Italy—clearly the work of a serial killer—authorities wonder: whose jurisdiction is it?

FBI Special Agent Adele Sharp—triple agent of the U.S., France and Germany—is called in as the only one capable of maneuvering the layers of authority and of tapping her brilliant mind to stop the killer.

But as more victims turn up—on other trains, in other countries—the case grows increasingly complex. Can this all be the work of one serial killer?

And if so, where will he strike next?

An action-packed mystery series of international intrigue and riveting suspense, LEFT TO LAPSE will have you turning pages late into the night.

Books #8-#10 are also available!

LEFT TO LAPSE
(An Adele Sharp Mystery—Book 7)

Did you know that I've written multiple novels in the mystery genre? If you haven't read all my series, click the image below to download a series starter!

Blake Pierce

Blake Pierce is the USA Today bestselling author of the RILEY PAGE mystery series, which includes seventeen books. Blake Pierce is also the author of the MACKENZIE WHITE mystery series, comprising fourteen books; of the AVERY BLACK mystery series, comprising six books; of the KERI LOCKE mystery series, comprising five books; of the MAKING OF RILEY PAIGE mystery series, comprising six books; of the KATE WISE mystery series, comprising seven books; of the CHLOE FINE psychological suspense mystery, comprising six books; of the JESSE HUNT psychological suspense thriller series, comprising fifteen books (and counting); of the AU PAIR psychological suspense thriller series, comprising three books; of the ZOE PRIME mystery series, comprising six books; of the ADELE SHARP mystery series, comprising ten books (and counting); of the EUROPEAN VOYAGE cozy mystery series, comprising six books (and counting); of the new LAURA FROST FBI suspense thriller, comprising three books (and counting); of the new ELLA DARK FBI suspense thriller, comprising three books (and counting); and of the new A YEAR IN EUROPE cozy mystery series, comprising three books (and counting).

An avid reader and lifelong fan of the mystery and thriller genres, Blake loves to hear from you, so please feel free to visit www.blakepierceauthor.com to learn more and stay in touch.

BOOKS BY BLAKE PIERCE

A YEAR IN EUROPE
A MURDER IN PARIS (Book #1)
DEATH IN FLORENCE (Book #2)
VENGEANCE IN VIENNA (Book #3)

ELLA DARK FBI SUSPENSE THRILLER
GIRL, GONE (Book #1)
GIRL, TAKEN (Book #2)
GIRL, HUNTED (Book #3)

LAURA FROST FBI SUSPENSE THRILLER
ALREADY GONE (Book #1)
ALREADY SEEN (Book #2)
ALREADY TRAPPED (Book #3)

EUROPEAN VOYAGE COZY MYSTERY SERIES
MURDER (AND BAKLAVA) (Book #1)
DEATH (AND APPLE STRUDEL) (Book #2)
CRIME (AND LAGER) (Book #3)
MISFORTUNE (AND GOUDA) (Book #4)
CALAMITY (AND A DANISH) (Book #5)
MAYHEM (AND HERRING) (Book #6)

ADELE SHARP MYSTERY SERIES
LEFT TO DIE (Book #1)
LEFT TO RUN (Book #2)
LEFT TO HIDE (Book #3)
LEFT TO KILL (Book #4)
LEFT TO MURDER (Book #5)
LEFT TO ENVY (Book #6)
LEFT TO LAPSE (Book #7)
LEFT TO VANISH (Book #8)
LEFT TO HUNT (Book #9)
LEFT TO FEAR (Book #10)

THE AU PAIR SERIES
ALMOST GONE (Book#1)
ALMOST LOST (Book #2)

ALMOST DEAD (Book #3)

ZOE PRIME MYSTERY SERIES
FACE OF DEATH (Book#1)
FACE OF MURDER (Book #2)
FACE OF FEAR (Book #3)
FACE OF MADNESS (Book #4)
FACE OF FURY (Book #5)
FACE OF DARKNESS (Book #6)

A JESSIE HUNT PSYCHOLOGICAL SUSPENSE SERIES
THE PERFECT WIFE (Book #1)
THE PERFECT BLOCK (Book #2)
THE PERFECT HOUSE (Book #3)
THE PERFECT SMILE (Book #4)
THE PERFECT LIE (Book #5)
THE PERFECT LOOK (Book #6)
THE PERFECT AFFAIR (Book #7)
THE PERFECT ALIBI (Book #8)
THE PERFECT NEIGHBOR (Book #9)
THE PERFECT DISGUISE (Book #10)
THE PERFECT SECRET (Book #11)
THE PERFECT FAÇADE (Book #12)
THE PERFECT IMPRESSION (Book #13)
THE PERFECT DECEIT (Book #14)
THE PERFECT MISTRESS (Book #15)

CHLOE FINE PSYCHOLOGICAL SUSPENSE SERIES
NEXT DOOR (Book #1)
A NEIGHBOR'S LIE (Book #2)
CUL DE SAC (Book #3)
SILENT NEIGHBOR (Book #4)
HOMECOMING (Book #5)
TINTED WINDOWS (Book #6)

KATE WISE MYSTERY SERIES
IF SHE KNEW (Book #1)
IF SHE SAW (Book #2)
IF SHE RAN (Book #3)
IF SHE HID (Book #4)

IF SHE FLED (Book #5)
IF SHE FEARED (Book #6)
IF SHE HEARD (Book #7)

THE MAKING OF RILEY PAIGE SERIES
WATCHING (Book #1)
WAITING (Book #2)
LURING (Book #3)
TAKING (Book #4)
STALKING (Book #5)
KILLING (Book #6)

RILEY PAIGE MYSTERY SERIES
ONCE GONE (Book #1)
ONCE TAKEN (Book #2)
ONCE CRAVED (Book #3)
ONCE LURED (Book #4)
ONCE HUNTED (Book #5)
ONCE PINED (Book #6)
ONCE FORSAKEN (Book #7)
ONCE COLD (Book #8)
ONCE STALKED (Book #9)
ONCE LOST (Book #10)
ONCE BURIED (Book #11)
ONCE BOUND (Book #12)
ONCE TRAPPED (Book #13)
ONCE DORMANT (Book #14)
ONCE SHUNNED (Book #15)
ONCE MISSED (Book #16)
ONCE CHOSEN (Book #17)

MACKENZIE WHITE MYSTERY SERIES
BEFORE HE KILLS (Book #1)
BEFORE HE SEES (Book #2)
BEFORE HE COVETS (Book #3)
BEFORE HE TAKES (Book #4)
BEFORE HE NEEDS (Book #5)
BEFORE HE FEELS (Book #6)
BEFORE HE SINS (Book #7)
BEFORE HE HUNTS (Book #8)

BEFORE HE PREYS (Book #9)
BEFORE HE LONGS (Book #10)
BEFORE HE LAPSES (Book #11)
BEFORE HE ENVIES (Book #12)
BEFORE HE STALKS (Book #13)
BEFORE HE HARMS (Book #14)

AVERY BLACK MYSTERY SERIES
CAUSE TO KILL (Book #1)
CAUSE TO RUN (Book #2)
CAUSE TO HIDE (Book #3)
CAUSE TO FEAR (Book #4)
CAUSE TO SAVE (Book #5)
CAUSE TO DREAD (Book #6)

KERI LOCKE MYSTERY SERIES
A TRACE OF DEATH (Book #1)
A TRACE OF MUDER (Book #2)
A TRACE OF VICE (Book #3)
A TRACE OF CRIME (Book #4)
A TRACE OF HOPE (Book #5)

Made in the USA
Las Vegas, NV
04 September 2022